OLDE
MYSTERIUM

Douglas Patten

OLDE

MYSTERIUM

Published by:
Literati Press
13114 114th Lane NE
Kirkland, WA 98034

International Standard Book Number: 978-0-9857985-0-5

Printed in the United States of America

Photograph on cover by Len Saltiel, www.lensaltiel.com

Cover design by Caitlin Patten & Douglas Patten

Page layout by Douglas Patten

for

Caitlin

CHAPTER ONE

THE FACE LOOKING back at Daniel was grizzled, unshaven and sad. His head, once flush with wavy brown locks was now cropped short and sparser than he remembered it yesterday, and seemed much more befitting an older man. He glanced down at his physique, not young but certainly not out of shape—just not what it was in his twenties. Daniel finally looked into his own gray eyes, looking grayer back at him and he sighed. He stepped away from the mirror.

A single brown satchel sat alone on the bed, full of the belongings he would take with him. Hoisting it over his shoulder, he raked the room to see if there was anything else he would take. Framed wedding pictures and other memorabilia of happy times sat displayed around the room. He wanted nothing to do with any of it.

At the bottom of the stairs Dan approached the front door but stopped with a side glance into the living room where a grimacing blonde woman sat with her arms folded. Her blue eyes pierced him with their glistening, red stare; they betrayed her true emotion: grief. Even in her emotional depths she still retained a core of beauty that shown so brightly in their wedding photos. He wanted to look away but forced himself to meet her gaze. It was as if he stared at the sun.

"I didn't hear you come in," Dan said.

She looked at his satchel. "Are you leaving then?"

He nodded and bit back the words full of bile forming on his tongue.

"Where will you go?"

"It shouldn't matter to you."

She brushed a golden tress behind her ear. "It does matter to me Dan."

"Bullshit." Dan walked over to the fridge and pulled out a can of Coke, placing it in his jacket pocket.

"Dan, I wish you would rethink this."

"Rethink what?" Dan felt the anger well up and he could hold back the dogs of war no longer. "I wish I could rethink about being married to you. I wish I could slap myself awake from it all on our wedding day five years ago."

"That's not fair." A tear ejected from Bridgette's eye and ran down her cheek. "I love you Daniel!"

"Goddammit Bridgette! I'm not leaving because you claim to love me. I'm not leaving because our finances are trashed. I'm not even leaving because I've been out of work for a year." Dan leaned forward over the counter, leveling his gaze at her. "I'm leaving because I was supposed to be able to trust you; and you kicked me while I was down. Like a dog."

"It was a mistake Daniel! And I'm sorry you had to find out about it." She sat down and placed her head in her hands.

"You bet it was a mistake. Your mistake caused me to look real hard at what a mistake our marriage has been." He stopped but couldn't stand the tension, so he grabbed the nearest glass on the counter and threw it across the room where it shattered upon the wall. A hundred diamond shards sprayed everywhere.

Bridgette's body shook in shock and then followed into full, convulsing sobs. "Please stop, I still love you. I love you Daniel!"

"How can I possibly believe that?" He said.

Bridgette shrugged her shoulders.

"I can't stay here in this damned place with you! It's all lost, don't you get that? It's over." Dan walked toward the front door but before he could reach the knob, Bridgette fell on her knees in front of him, hugging his legs.

"Don't go! I don't want to be alone."

Daniel shook her loose and she fell back onto the carpet. "But you're not alone. You have *him*."

"Please Daniel," she sobbed. "I'm so sorry. So sorry. Please don't. I love you."

Daniel stepped forward and opened the front door. Without so much as a glance back he spoke: "Damn you."

The rain tapped upon his head in an arrhythmic beat, the music of chaos. Daniel loved it and was thankful he lived in a city that saw plenty of it. The bus stop stood vacant and he didn't mind. He looked at his watch; the metro was running five minutes behind but there was nowhere he could go where he would end up late. Wherever Daniel landed, he would be on time. Most of his friends had been coworkers at the Seattle Post-Intelligencer, and like him, most of them had also fallen upon hard times since the paper ceased to print. It was a cost saving measure instituted by the corporate owners who insisted that a website would be more beneficial to the bottom line than printing. It was not a new story, or even a newsworthy story—newspapers were hurting all over the country. Dan was among a battalion of unemployed journalists. The Seattle Times had tried to pick up some slack and hired a handful of the migrating writers and editors, but their budget was doing nary better than their once formidable competitor, the Seattle P.I.

The metro bus pulled to the curb and Daniel climbed aboard, running his passenger card through the entry terminal.

"Where you headed?" the driver asked.

Dan's mind went blank. "Pioneer Square." It was the first thing to roll off his tongue.

The bus left the curb, slowly gaining momentum as it careened against the rain. Daniel scanned the bus to find a seat that would give him solitude and space to think. The bus was hardly full, a handful of passengers at most. He treaded down the aisle until he found two empty seats where he set down his satchel and reclined, his face turned toward the rain-pelted window—eyeing the darkened skies. Three teenage boys behind him at the back of the bus entertained themselves, guffawing and waxing innuendos. Daniel paid no mind but pulled himself and all of his focus inward. Everything around him disappeared into the periphery until there was only him and the rain on the other side of the window.

Daniel thought of his book. It was something he initially imagined, toyed with, kept notes on, and eventually he began to write it. Finding time to write at home had been difficult while at the P.I., but after being let go time turned into sand slipping through his fingers. He couldn't understand where it had gone, or the energy to follow through on the keyboard. He found himself sleeping later and later into the day, making it all but impossible to spend time with Bridgette when she would come home from work. Then there were days where he couldn't even remember seeing her at all. He would climb into bed the moment she woke up and he would rise again as she was getting ready to turn in. But it all came to a startled halt at the grim reckoning of his marriage. He knew things had been far from Shangri-La but had not expected to be brought down to Sheol—from heaven to hell in a matter of months. His heart told him he deeply loved Bridgette, but his mind could not reconcile how to begin to repair the damage done. Daniel once heard that the heart was eighteen inches from the head and he now wondered if that was the length of the divide between heaven and hell. He knew it was, at least for him.

Daniel's eyes focused through the showers outside to see a large globe spinning on its axis atop the building of the Seattle P.I., the mocking blue orb dancing upon the grave of his career. His lungs burned and Daniel realized he'd been holding his breath, but for what he did not know. There was no longer anything for which to hold it.

The noise behind Daniel was now raucous and so he turned to see the cause. The teens prodded a young homeless man. His hair was shaggy and his coat well worn. One of the boys snatched away his hat, smelling it and contorting his face into grotesque displeasure for the amusement of his friends. The man tried not to be bothered and said nothing but simply glared at the teens. Daniel looked forward but the bus driver was occupied with the road.

"Give it back," Daniel said. He didn't know why he did it. Maybe it was out of pity for the man, or maybe it was out of fear that he could become that man in the tattered coat. Daniel was after all a man with no place to go.

"Or what?" the leader of the boys replied, his chin thrust into the air.

Daniel said nothing. He had not planned this out.

One of the friends looked at Dan and then the homeless man. "Just give it back, man."

"No."

"Come on Aaron, just give the hobo back his hat," the friend said.

Aaron reached up and pulled on the cord, where a bell rang over the intercom. The bus pulled over to the curb and all three boys stood up. Aaron sneered and then threw the hat in the homeless man's lap. "Freak."

Each of the boys filed out, with Aaron being last. His youthful eyes were fired with discontent and were ever focused on Daniel until the bus left the curb and began again down the street.

Daniel glanced over at the tattered brown jacket and then the man's face. He couldn't be any older than thirty and yet he could see the creases where life on the street had weathered the young man's skin not unlike the jacket. "Are you all right?" Dan asked.

The man shrugged. "Sure."

Daniel noticed that the man would not look at him directly, scanning everything but Daniel's own face. He didn't know what else to say and so he settled back into his seat. His eyes glazed over and he retreated again back into his own head, allowing his thoughts to spin their web.

The bus again pulled over to the curb. "Excuse me, sir?"

Daniel looked up and caught the eyes of the driver in his rear view mirror.

"Pioneer Square? Here we are."

"Oh, right," Dan said and gathered his things, stepping off the bus back into the arrhythmic beating of the rain, walking down the street to nowhere.

CHAPTER TWO

DANIEL STOOD IN the rain, curbside, watching the bus peel away back into the traffic and disappear around the next corner. Leaving everything behind was not easy and watching the bus vanish was the last of it. He sighed and hitched his satchel up over his shoulder, stepping forward into the unknown and onward into the abyss of downtown Seattle. The rain continued to tap on his head and he flipped the collar up on his brown leather jacket in response. His thoughts returned to the bus and the young homeless man still on it. Dan wondered how long it would take before his own jacket became as weather-beaten as that man's had been.

His eyes traveled across the street to the old black iron pergola shielding a couple of benches from the downpour and he made his way there, sitting and wondering what to do next. Dan pulled out his wallet and looked inside, confirming the five dollars, two credit cards, and a bank card he had left. He watched the busy cars pushing through the rain and then he saw the various people walking by; more than a few were carrying backpacks with what he assumed were their only earthly belongings. One woman pushed a shopping cart loaded with rubbish into a vacant store front and began to unload the things she would need to sleep there. Dan could see evening was approaching and watched the woman go through her ritual of laying out her sleeping bag and position her cart of possessions against the wall behind her so she could protect them through the night.

"What am I doing?" he said under his breath. "I don't belong here." Yet all the same he knew it was a lie. This was exactly where he belonged; there was nowhere else to go. Fear crept into his stomach and sat there like bile, eating at his soul. He wanted to do anything to feel normal. A Starbucks faced him from across the street warming the wet sidewalk outside with its warm, brown glow from within.

Daniel stood up and crossed the street, standing outside the shop and looking inward at the happy people cradling their warm moments of bliss in white paper cups. His hand reached out and opened the door, and he stepped inside. He stood back for a moment, wondering what to do, but nobody even looked his way. Dan realized it was because he still looked like a normal guy and not like a bum...at least not yet anyway. He stepped up to the counter.

"How may I help you?" The happy voice of the barista behind the bar called to him. He resented her cheerfulness.

"Venti drip with room," he said and pulled out his wallet, handing over a credit card.

She took the card and ran it through her cashier station once, twice, and three times before handing it back. "I'm sorry but your card isn't providing a transaction."

Daniel sighed and pulled out another card, handing it over. The barista ran it though again, handing it back with the same result. Her eyes were still bright and happy but his were becoming sullen. He then handed her his only five dollar bill. "Sorry about that," he managed to say.

"No problem," she replied and handed him back a sparse handful of change and a venti, white paper cup.

Daniel added sugar and cream to his coffee and then found a quiet corner table to sit at. He laid down his satchel and sipped his own moment of bliss, wondering if he would ever be able to do this again. He raked his gaze across the rest of the coffee shop's patrons, trying to guess what they were each thinking and doing and wondering where they each lived and what kind of homes they would eventually be heading towards. His mind wandered everywhere except toward his own situation, trying to keep distracted at every expense for the moment because Daniel knew that once he stepped outside the doors of Starbucks he would have to find a place to sleep for the night.

He listened to the cool thrumming of a blues guitar over the speakers and imagined what it would be like to play like that. To have the ease of a talent that would let him express his feelings through music in such a sorrowful way. Daniel felt it and could understand how such a sad genre of music could attend the attention of thousands. He allowed the music to sink in and converse with his soul.

The barista stepped out from behind the counter and began approaching each table, saying something in a low voice. People nodded and began to get up and leave. She approached him; the moment of his dread was at hand.

"I'm so sorry, but we have to close the store," she said when she came to his table. Daniel nodded and spoke an empty thank you while hitching up his satchel and heading toward the front door.

The rain outside tapped on his head and shoulders again as he began the search for a spot to bed down for the night. He sauntered down the sidewalk, his eyes darting from side to side searching for a place sheltered from the rain and unoccupied by the other homeless citizens. Finally he spotted an empty storefront that was well lit and he made his way toward it.

Daniel sat down in a dry corner and laid his satchel between himself and the wall. He opened up his bag and began to paw through it, making sure everything he packed was there, but more so just to keep busy. Two shirts, a pair of jeans, two pairs of underwear, two pairs of socks, and his favorite book *The Pillars of the Earth* by Ken Follett. He had read it many times before it ever became the popular icon of Oprah's book club. Somehow it brought him comfort but he didn't feel like reading at the moment. Then his hand fell upon an unfamiliar rectangular object and he pulled it out: a framed wedding picture. Daniel had not packed it but he could easily surmise Bridgette had done so while he had been in the bathroom. The photo displayed a happy couple that Daniel no longer recognized. The whites of their smiles shone brighter than the wedding dress and their happiness jogged a flash of memories before him, but he stopped it before the pain could resurface. It was a life he couldn't live any longer and it was a love that died; a dead dream never to return. He didn't have the energy to get up and find a trash can into which he could deposit the frame and so he just placed it back in the satchel. Daniel thought about leaving it on the street, which seemed befitting, but somehow he couldn't bring himself to do it.

His hand reached into his jacket pocket and he found the can of Coke. The coffee was dinner. The soda would be for breakfast. Dan laid his head against the brick wall and closed his eyes.

CHAPTER THREE

DANIEL'S OLD BROWN satchel was hitched firmly over his shoulder as he walked. Pioneer Square was arguably the oldest part of Seattle. Ruddy brick buildings with their jutting fronts dominated the sidewalk. Yet he didn't notice as the morning continued to blur around him.

His eyes peered into the Starbucks from the night before filled with more happy patrons. He longed to join them but knew he didn't have the funds. Next door, a bar bustled with sports fans who had recently vacated Qwest Field, celebrating the latest victory of the Sounders FC with rousing rounds of beer and song. Daniel walked past and left his envy behind. Finally, on the corner sat a brick building not unlike the rest and yet strangely peaceful amidst the business of the square.

His eyes scrolled upward and found a rain beaten sign proclaiming *Olde Mysterium Books & Oddities*. Reading was the easiest way to escape from reality into serenity or adventure, and if there was ever a time he needed to escape it was now. He cupped his hand up against the window and leaned forward, looking inside. It was quiet, there were no shoppers and no booksellers on the floor, just heavy wooden racks filled with old volumes.

Daniel figured at least he could leave the rain, if only for a moment. He opened the large oak front door, causing a bell to ring overhead but no one approached him. The interior smelled of old paper and hardwood…an unusually pleasant combination. Daniel could tell someone else was in the back of the store but he didn't bother to seek them out. Instead he investigated the nearest rack of books. Most were old hardbacks that had seen better days, many of which were titles unfamiliar to him even though he had a decent working knowledge of literature: *The First and Second Books of Enoch, The Divine Pymander, The Sepher Yetzirah*…and the list continued onward. Daniel had hardly a clue what they were about and he couldn't find any signs pointing to any sort of organization or cataloging.

"May I help you?"

The voice startled Daniel and he turned to see a man with wisps of white hair sticking out over his ears and circling around his bald, brown pate. The man was old and yet his frail frame did nothing to hide the vibrancy behind his black eyes. Daniel could not tell what his accent was, but guessed it was Middle Eastern.

"What?" Dan said.

"Are you looking for something containing the great mysteries?" the man said, motioning to the rack of books in front of them.

"Uh, not really. No."

The man nodded. His thin hair waving, as if by a breeze. "Understandable. People today are far more concerned with the next football game or the next movie release...or the next great getaway from the drabness of life. The search for entertainment overcoming the search for knowledge. So what *are* you looking for?"

"Actually I was just curious. What is this place?" Dan asked.

The man's thin hand waved over the store. "This is a lifetime of collected knowledge. The secrets of the ages."

Daniel's spine tensed, feeling uncomfortable but his curiosity nagged onward. "You've read every book in here?"

The man nodded. "Most of them twice."

"Wow." Daniel scratched his chin. "So what do they say?"

The old man's smile was slightly wolfish. "Nothing mostly. Every book in here contains small gems of wisdom buried within pages of rubbish. Every book except one."

Daniel's eyebrows arched upward. "Which one?"

"It is a book in which every page reveals something deep about the human heart. Our deficiencies as well as our road to triumph. Perhaps one day you'll discover it for yourself. For me to tell you would indeed be an injustice."

Daniel caught a laugh in his throat. What an old coot. He owned the bookstore and yet he was uninterested in promoting any of them. "So knowledge is rubbish?"

"No, knowledge is knowledge. The more we seem to know, the less we understand."

Now Dan felt playful. "Then why is all of this knowledge so great? I have an excellent education, but it has done nothing for me except fill my head with facts to regurgitate. Knowledge can't even help me find a job."

The old man shook his head. "Knowledge does not make us great. Neither does wealth, power, a career, the fast car, the big house, or any of the myriad paths offered by this world. There is only one thing that makes us great."

"Uh huh." Dan backed away toward the front door and opened it. The bell chimed overhead. "Well look, this has been interesting but…"

"Young man. Where ever you are going—I hope you find what you are looking for. This has been the most pleasant conversation I've had in quite a while. Please visit again." The old man smiled, this time with genuine sincerity.

Daniel nodded and left.

The rain resumed tapping upon his head. The bookstore had not been the brief refuge for which he hoped. His encounter with the owner was uncomfortable. Daniel smiled. What a crazy old man. The mysteries of the ages had long since been surpassed by the development of science and the advent of technology. There were so few mysteries left in life he wondered if there were any left to discover.

Daniel made his way through the square, through the soggy air. There was some comfort to being caught in the rain, it was a kind of anonymity not provided in any other sort of weather and yet a slice of his soul desired strongly not to be left alone. He looked back to see the store. It looked lonely amidst the crowded buildings, as if shunned to the corner by its busier and lively neighbors. He hitched up his satchel and turned his collar up again against the rain. His eyes gazed upward and saw that the sky which had once been gray was now deep charcoal and the street lights flipped on one at a time, sensing the darkness as he did. He knew there was a shelter nearby as he had written an article on it two years before. His lips formed a grim line as he remembered interviewing the caretaker on the shortage of space during the holidays, especially during times of economic distress. At the time he had smugly considered his incredible fortune at being able to have a warm home to go to every night instead of requiring the necessity of finding a spare cot. He shook his head, realizing it was that necessity which had become his eventuality. Dan shuffled forward toward the Union Gospel Mission, hoping Jack Polanski, the caretaker would remember him.

Yet what caught him in his tracks was the tingling right between his eyes followed by a shiver in his spine. He sensed someone behind him, but before he could turn his head to see, Daniel was struck behind the head and fell to the ground. His hands instinctively cradled his throbbing skull as he looked up and saw Aaron and the two other boys from the bus glowering over him like predators.

"I recognized you," Aaron said. "You're that nosey douche from the bus." He kicked Dan in the ribs. "Mind your own business next time."

And with that, the boys started kicking and stomping. Pain was everywhere in Daniel's body, but the only thing he could do was curl up and cover his head. Each assault shook his nerves with fresh agony, and yet he was helpless to do anything. There was no running, no fighting back. Just the ground and their feet hammering his ribs and back. Dan tried to plea with them, but each time he opened his mouth instead of words there was only the wretched sounds of his distress.

The darkness crept in through the periphery of his vision, eventually overcoming his eyesight and pulling him down and deeper within. Almost like sleep. Down…deeper.

CHAPTER FOUR

SOMEWHERE A CHIME rang, the high tone and brassy timbre carrying into space. Daniel opened his eyes upon an old room with a plaster ceiling and paneled walls. He turned his head but the searing pain in his neck and back caught him.

"Lie still." The voice was caring and wizened with the slightest lilt of an Arabic accent.

Dan tried to move again to see who...but the pain wracked his ribcage.

"My son, I said lie still." The little old man from the crazy bookstore now stood over him. His black eyes held an abundance of caring and caused Daniel to acquiesce, loosening his tension and letting out the breath bound tightly in his chest. "My deepest apologies for your confusion. Please allow me to rectify this by introducing myself. My name is Saba Ghazal. You are now safe."

"Daniel." Dan said with his weakened voice and not without a mustered effort.

The old man smiled with his long, white teeth. "There's no need to speak either, unless you must of course, Daniel." He lifted a rag from a steaming basin and used the wet warmth to wipe over Dan's face. "You may rest here for as long as you like. My understanding is that you are not in any rush to get anywhere."

Daniel's brow pulled together, scrunching his forehead and he opened his mouth to speak but stopped.

The old man held up the picture frame with Daniel and Bridgette, their smiles now marred by the cracked pane spiderwebbing within the framed borders. A befitting description of his marriage and his life. "There's no need to explain," Saba said. "The young ruffians who did this to you took your bag, but not before they tossed this out." He placed the picture on a side table next to the bed. "In my opinion, they served you the honor of leaving your best possession."

"No. They left me my pain."

"Pain is useful," Saba said, now wiping away the muck and blood from Daniel's arms and chest. The warmth helped Daniel resist the urge to wince at the cleansing of every sore spot. "Pain keeps us grounded in reality; otherwise we would all drift off into self invented fantasies, never realizing our full potential."

"Well, my reality sucks right now," Dan spat out. "Any potential I had was left behind."

Saba gave a tight lipped chuckle. "That is where you and I disagree. We all retain the greatest of potential, whether we realize it or not is hardly the question."

Daniel's eyes closed. "Potential for what? I can't even see past my own broken heart let alone see anything else I have left. I just don't believe I can do it anymore."

"The potential lies within each of us to affect those around us in a positive way. Therein lies the key to a successful life, Daniel. A life well lived is a life well given in love. It doesn't matter whether you believe in yourself...not so long as there are others who believe in you. And I for one, believe."

Saba had finished wiping away the beating from Daniel's body and now lent his hands to pull him into an upright sitting position. His withered hand motioned toward a bathroom. "The shower is yours, if you would like to finish cleaning up by yourself."

Daniel nodded but winced from the pounding within his skull.

"There is a fresh robe in there for you as well while your clothes are washed. When you are finished, would you please join me downstairs? The coffee's hot."

Daniel smiled. "Sure." And he went into the bathroom, stripping off the rest of his mucky clothing, turning the water to hot and stepping in, allowing the radiating heat to splash against him and melt away the chill. It was the first thing he was able to appreciate in an otherwise gray, disheartening day.

After the shower, he dried off and put on the robe, thick and white and warm. The mirror reflected a face he hardly recognized, marred by cuts, scrapes, and bruises. Stepping out of the bathroom, he found a pair of slippers waiting for him by the door.

"Daniel," Saba's voice called from outside the bedroom. "Could you please carry the rest of your clothing downstairs so that it could join the laundry?"

Daniel put on the slippers and gathered the wet remains of his clothing from the bathroom down the stairwell outside the bedroom. It was old and wooden. Each creak and groan beneath his feet betrayed the age of the building, but there was something comforting in it. At the base of the stairs, he realized he had been in an apartment above *Olde Mysterium*. He looked out over the stacks of books, searching for Saba but the old man appeared directly before him with his hands out. "I'll take those. This way my son."

It was then a thought struck Daniel and he couldn't help but ask. "How did you get me in here?"

"Not without a great deal of effort, I'm afraid, but I had some help from Billy Pints the barkeep next door."

"Oh. Well, did you happen to see anything? Maybe where those fuckers went?"

Saba shook his head and placed the rest of Daniel's clothes into the washer, starting the load. "No. I came out and saw the tail end of it. Would you believe that before I got to you, something odd happened?" He then led Dan to a table already set with two steaming mugs of coffee.

"Really?"

"Yes. There were two men who witnessed, what I could only assume, was your whole event. But it's not that they witnessed it that mattered, but rather who witnessed it that is curious." Saba said and sipped his coffee. "One was a doctor I know who has an office near here. The other was a well known judge who presides at the courthouse just up the block."

Daniel's eyes were wide. He poured some cream and sugar into his coffee, stirring it. "Did they call the police?"

Saba shook his head. "No, they walked away."

"I suppose that makes you my good Samaritan. Thank you Saba," Dan said and lifted the coffee to his lips.

"Exactly," Saba said, his black eyes shining like two jewels. "It was my potential to affect you in a positive way. There was no mistake in you walking into my store today, Daniel. There are no coincidences. I believe our meeting was predestined, what could easily be called a *divine appointment.*"

Dan shook his head. "A divine appointment, so you could save my life?"

Saba shrugged. "I don't know about saving your life, but it seems that we can both mutually benefit each other."

"How?"

"I am an old man and I own a store in need of some repairs...refinishing the floor, rebuilding shelves and such. I understand that you are in need of a job. Do you have any experience in any such matters?" Saba arched one bushy eyebrow.

"When I was younger I used to help my father with finishing carpentry. Though it's been a long time," Dan said.

The old man smiled. "You're hired. And you can also use the flat above the store until you are ready to find something else. Truth be told, I need someone here at night to keep an eye on everything. There are a great many valuable books in here."

Dan's heart leapt in his chest. "Thank you…I don't know how to thank you. I don't really believe in fate, or destiny, but…"

"A divine appointment? Yes, I believe it is, Daniel."

CHAPTER FIVE

THE ALARM BUZZED, pulling Daniel away from the warm fuzziness of sleep into the solid reality of a new day. His eyes opened and gazed about the cozy apartment, furnished only with the bed he was in, a nightstand, and a small but ornate table with two matching chairs. The window betrayed the still dusk of early morning, preparing to turn ever more towards the light of day.

Daniel pulled himself upright from the soft bed. It was smaller than what he had been used to and yet he found last night's sleep among the most restful of his life. The wedding picture stood up on the nightstand, posed in its fractured splendor. Dan grimaced and went to the bathroom to splash some water on his face. Beside the sink was a fresh toothbrush and new tube of

paste, laying there as if they had read the thoughts of
his mind.

He freshened up and put on his only set of clean
clothes before making his way down the staircase, each
footfall catalyzing a creak or groan from the floorboards
beneath. It made him smile. At the base of the stairs, he
could see immediately that the lights were already on
and yet he remembered turning them off the night
before. In a cautious voice he called out, "Saba?"

"Over here my boy. We're not open yet and so I
hoped you would join me for breakfast."

Daniel approached an opening at the rear of the
store surrounded by the racks of books. A reading table
with two chairs sat upon the stately bold colors of a
Turkish rug.

"Take a seat. Take a seat Daniel," Saba came over
to the table and motioned to the seat opposite before
sitting down himself.

The table was spread with fruit, hardboiled eggs,
buttered toast…and of course coffee. Daniel sat and
watched Saba load his plate before following suit, and
yet he couldn't help but notice the old man close his
eyes for the briefest moment before his first bite. Dan
was not interested in praying—to anyone much less
anything. The breakfast was filling and fresh.

"Do you have any suggestions on where to start?" Saba asked.

"With the store?" Dan said, his eyes gazing about the store. "The plaster is old and cracked in several places. I would like to see what's behind it so we can know what to do."

Saba nodded. "Fair enough. Any ideas?"

"Maybe. This building is old enough and my suspicion is that brick may be behind it all. If that's the case then I would suggest removing all the plaster and keeping the brick in its place. It would lend an authentic *mysterium* to the ambience of this place."

"Wonderful. I would have never thought of that," the old man said, sipping his black coffee.

"Also while I'm at it, your wiring is probably in need of replacement as well and would be easier to do once the plaster is removed. Have you thought about replacing the light fixtures in here?"

Saba shook his head.

Dan scratched his head and looked above. The current fixtures were simple fluorescents with gleaming white, cold light—designed to perfectly suck the juice from human eyeballs. "I might suggest removal of the current lighting and putting in something warmer instead."

Saba smiled. "Yes, I think that would be wonderful."

Daniel suddenly flushed, "I forgot to ask you, what is the budget we're working with?"

"No budget as of yet but I think what you have proposed is an excellent start. Thank you for your help Daniel. You were clearly a Godsend."

Daniel stood and began clearing away the dishes, bringing them to the kitchen behind the small office. Saba gathered the rest of everything from the table and followed. Daniel rinsed the dishes and handed them to the old man, who loaded them into the dishwasher. When they were done, Daniel noticed that Saba stood there looking at him. Waiting.

"I uh, should get to work then," Dan said.

Saba nodded with a thin smile. "Lunch is at noon."

Daniel pulled apart the plaster, peeling it away from the brick wall beneath. A small leap of joy within him at being right about the brick assisted in quickening the pace of his work. He knew that *Olde Mysterium* would be given a new life with a new look. For the first time in a long while, Daniel finally felt useful. The plaster drying out the skin on his hands felt like nothing compared to the ecstatic imaginings of the store's new interior. He realized that he had not felt this pleased with himself since he had worked with his father so many years ago, and yet there were so many hurtful memories close to the surface there as well.

He set those hurts aside as he continued to pull at the ever cracking plaster coming away beneath the strain of his hands. He knew deep in his core that somehow manual labor was fulfilling in a way years at a desk job could never compare.

Daniel looked down at himself covered in a thin layer of white dust and wall particles. The bell chimed and he knew that someone had walked into the store. His eyes turned to see, wondering who else in the world would come into such an arcane store as this one. He noticed a young lady about his same age with black curly hair bobbing up and down in a tightly pulled ponytail as she walked through the book racks with confidence. She was attractive in a sharp featured sort of way and still shared in the wiry exuberance of youth that Daniel felt he had left behind. She didn't even glance his way.

"Saba," she called out.

"Over here Deborah."

She met the old man at the back of the store and they spoke quietly as he handed her a parcel wrapped in brown paper. Daniel guessed they were books but couldn't be sure. Then he realized he was watching out of mere curiosity and turned back to focus on his work.

The bell chimed again and he knew she had left.

Time passed in brief but laborious moments as Daniel pulled and pried the plaster loose from its ages old stronghold. He knew that it had been the vogue of design in its day, but the day of reckoning had come for the store and it would need to go through some loss to make it new. Daniel loved the idea of taking old things —broken things, and making them new. There was something fresh about a new start that appealed to the appetite of his soul, and so the overflowing vigor from within flowed outward to his hands as he continued to break the chalky wall and peel it away to expose the red, raw brick beneath.

It was only Saba's voice from below that broke the chord of focus ringing within Daniel's mind. "You've covered quite a bit of distance already."

Daniel smiled. "I'm motivated."

"Motivation is good if it comes from within. Motivation from without, however..."

Daniel turned to see the old man shelving books below, working around the drop cloth overlaying the bookcases directly beneath the wall demolition. "What do you mean?"

"I'm saying it is that which lives within us is infinitely more powerful—and good—than that which inhabits the world around us."

Daniel shook his head. "I still don't understand. Sometimes you speak in mysteries, why not just speak plainly?"

Saba stopped. "How familiar are you with the Bible?"

Now Daniel laughed. "Familiar enough to know to stay away from it."

"Indeed." A thin smile spread across Saba's lips. "Well then, if you don't mind me speaking about it…?"

"Go ahead."

"There is a reason why Jesus always told his greatest truths in parables; it was so those ready for the truth could find it and those who were unready, or unwilling, could leave it be or find it later. You see, Daniel, not all people are ready for their fantasies to be shattered by truth to expose the reality beneath it. It can be raw and painful, but coming to accept it eventually makes us more real and truly beautiful. That is what I meant. It is the raw and real you beneath that makes you unique and important, not the trappings of a well bred life designed to keep you insulated." Saba sighed and raised his hands. "Apologies. It just kind of gets away from me sometimes."

Daniel thought and then responded: "Unready or unwilling. But what if I believe in nothing?"

"Well," Saba scratched his chin. "The problem with those who don't believe isn't that they believe in nothing, but rather they will believe anything—because we are all designed to believe in *something*."

"There you go again," Dan called out as he dropped a large piece of wall onto the drop cloth below.

Saba smiled. "I suppose it comes from years of living alone and running a store filled with books nobody reads anymore. Many of them are collectible, but most will never be read by another person even if they are purchased. Mine are the ramblings of an eccentric old skinflint unable to share the knowledge very often."

"Honestly, I don't mind," Dan said.

"Thank you Daniel for your indulgence." Saba pulled a couple of more books from the cart and shelved them before speaking again. "Would you mind if I asked you a personal question?"

"I suppose it depends on the question."

Saba placed his index finger upon the dimple in his chin. "I would guess that you grew up under a churched influence of some kind. What soured your spirit?"

Daniel exhaled. This man, a stranger, was asking something very personal and painful, but Dan weighed it out, figuring it would be all right. The old man had cared for him the night before and Dan felt like he owed Saba something. "Growing up we went to church every Sunday, but there was something fake about it. My mother was loving but sad. Dad was a deacon in the church. Everything looked good from outside, and yet it was inside our home that was the problem. My father was a mean man."

Saba nodded gravely. "Alcohol?"

Dan shook his head. "No, he never drank anything. He would say 'alcohol has never passed these lips.'"

Saba chuckled. "Well, Jesus can't even hold a match to that."

"If I got a bad grade, he would fall into a rage and yell at me how I wasn't doing anything good enough. He said I was disappointing Jesus and then he would ground me to my room where I would take all of my meals until his anger dissipated, which could take days.

"There was one time that he locked me in my room for a whole summer," Dan said in a low voice.

"What could have caused that?" Saba said.

"I was fifteen and curious about girls. We couldn't even talk about sex. Not ever. Dad found a Playboy under my bed, and so he locked me in my room with nothing to read but the Bible so that I would learn to repent.

"Our church wasn't much better. Everything revolved around guilt and manipulation to get everyone to perform here, serve there, tithe so much and so often. Everyone seemed to talk a lot about Jesus but no one behaved like they believed it. After high school, I went to college and came home with total disbelief in all of that crap. I told Dad I couldn't believe in a god that could be so cruel and judgmental. I would rather take my chances alone. Dad told me to leave if I wanted to live like a pagan. So I did."

Saba shook his head. "It is all crap."

"Excuse me?"

"Crap, as you say. I don't believe in that god either. Manipulation, irrational control, and guilt are symptoms of a spiritual flaw, one that we all have, but all are absent from the God I follow. And he never controls those whom he loves."

"And whom does your God love?"

"Everyone. That is the gift of free will. We make our own choices and we can choose to love him back...or not."

"It's hard enough to love people, how can we expect to love a God we never see?"

"Just because you can't see him doesn't mean he's not there," Saba said.

"Sure," Dan nodded.

Saba scratched the pate of his bald brown head. "How about we think of this another way. Can you see gravity?"

Dan shook his head.

"That's right, but we can see its effects everywhere, allowing us to stand upright, to build houses upon a firm foundation, to pool water for drinking or swimming. The direct effects of gravity are all around us and yet we cannot see it but we cannot deny its powerful force."

"I suppose so," Dan said.

"God is certainly at work in our world, all around us, each and every day. Make no mistake my son, we cannot see him but we cannot deny his powerful force affecting our world and even our very lives."

"All right, so if God is such a powerful force, then how come such terrible things happen? Why doesn't he just stop it? And I'm not even talking about the small things, but the biggies like rape, murder, genocide."

Saba held up his hand and motioned Daniel down from the ladder. "I want to show you something." He showed Daniel to the only reading nook in the store, tucked neatly away for privacy. On the wall hung a beautiful gilded frame but it was the treasure displayed inside that mastered Daniel's attention. A small strip of a scroll containing tiny but artfully scripted words in Hebrew filled the parchment.

"What is it?" Daniel asked.

"It's not what it is that matters, but the story of what it has gone through." Saba said. "This old but well preserved piece is just a fragment from a scroll of the Torah—the first five books of the bible which God gave to Moses upon the top of Mount Sinai. This particular Torah scroll was created in Germany during the late eighteenth century, right around the time of the American Revolution. The scroll itself was preserved through many wars that ravaged Europe until World War II when it was discovered by the Nazis and the rest of the scroll was destroyed." Saba said. "You see Daniel, this scroll fragment is a reminder of our free will. Humanity's pain is not derived from God nor is it caused by his absence or a failure to save us from pain. Our pain comes solely from the horrible things we do to one another, God is not absent, he is there witnessing everything but will not hinder our free will to affect each other, either for good or bad. And yet, he does everything possible to transform that pain into love so that we may heal ourselves and then heal others."

Daniel's eyes studied the beautifully unfamiliar letters. "What does it say?"

Saba's fingers reached out and touched the glass protecting the scroll fragment. "That's really the curious part. You see, for everything the entire scroll went through right on down to its destruction by the Nazis, to have this portion survive is rather curious indeed." Saba's shiny black eyes trained upon Daniel's inquisitive glare. "These are the ten commandments. The ultimate expression of our free will complete with guidelines to follow. God allowed the free will of men to destroy this copy of the word he breathed, but preserved the one piece that is his penultimate expression of our free will. If he can do something like this for a ratty piece of parchment, then just imagine what God is willing to do for those of us created in his image."

CHAPTER SIX

DANIEL STEPPED THROUGH the door of *Olde Mysterium* and surveyed the store as if apprising the lump of coal that he knew contained the diamond within. The plaster from the walls and ceiling had been torn out and the brick behind was cleaned up. He could see what it was going to become.

"Back from your walk so soon?" Saba said stepping from behind one of the book racks. His frail stature was dwarfed by the immense hardwood structures.

Daniel nodded and eyes travelled over top of the old man's head to rest upon a set of boxes behind him. "Are those…?"

"Ah, yes they are," Saba clapped his hands together. "The light fixtures. Open them open them."

Daniel tore open the boxes as if a child on Christmas. A part of him flittered at the thought of replacing the dingy old fluorescent bulbs withering the life out of everything. They were exactly as he hoped for: a simple lighting system that would suspend tracks down from the ceiling upon which would be affixed halogen bulbs, pointing light into any which direction. It would be soft, warm, comfortable and sublime. "When should I start?"

Saba laughed. "Tomorrow. Start tomorrow, but for now we need to close up the shop. I brought supper tonight."

It was then when the spicy scent assailed Daniel's nose and his stomach rumbled. He hadn't eaten anything since his thin breakfast. "Smells delicious."

"Cioppino. It's a shame to live in a place so bountiful with sea food if we don't eat it."

Daniel and Saba locked the front door and turned off the store lights, leaving on only the lights in the back, where the table was already set. They sat down and ladled the spicy red broth brimming with shellfish into their two modest bowls. Saba bowed his head for the briefest moment and then spooned into the soup. Daniel also bowed his head out of respect, but didn't quite know what to say—even in his head, but then he too tucked into the dinner. Fresh French bread, with its crackling skin and springy interior added to the meal as a means to sop the left over broth. Each of them had two full bowls in silence, enjoying the peace.

"Marvelous," Saba said, sitting back in his chair and placing his hands over the small bulge of his belly.

Daniel chuckled. "Very good indeed. How did you make that?"

"With about thirty dollars and a delivery by The Spaghetti House. It was the dish du jour."

Daniel smiled. "I'll have to remember that." And then something occurred to him.

"What is it?" Saba read the expression on his face.

"I know we eat together a lot, and there are no complaints because we eat well..."

The old man caught on, laughed and finished the thought, "but you wonder why I don't go home to eat with family?"

Daniel nodded.

"Well," Saba said scratching his chin, "I suppose sharing that part of my life with you now is best. Once, a long time ago when I lived in Lebanon, I did have a family. We worked hard, loved each other, and did our best not to draw any attention. In short we were merely surviving, and doing well at it."

"Why just surviving? Lebanon isn't a poor nation," Dan said.

Saba held his hands out as if weighing something invisible like a scale. "It is not poor in the sense that you make it out to be, but there are things about it that are dire indeed. You see Daniel, except for the western nations, most of the world's Christian population is downtrodden and exploited. Lebanon was no different in my time there. The intense hatred and—I believe the popular word is bigotry—against Christian people is almost entirely beyond bearing, and unreported, and yet they still seem to survive. This was during 1982 when many terrible things were happening to people I knew and loved. There were forced conversions and executions to follow if remaining unconverted. There was so much brutality that almost every day I would hear of a friend or family member being beaten to within one fraction of their life, and sometimes not even spared that."

Daniel's eyes were wide and his brow scrunched into layers of concern. "Why didn't the police help?"

"The police in those countries often turn a blind eye to minority mistreatment...and sometimes they instigate it. It's not like it is here, my son. There are no armies of lawyers seeking to petition the courts about racism, sexism, or religious discrimination. And even if there were, the courts are sympathetic with the aggressors."

"It seems hard to believe," Daniel said.

"Such is the way in most of the world, Daniel. Our land is an exception to the rule," Saba nodded. "Believe it because I have lived it."

Daniel sighed an expletive, running his fingers through his hair. "What happened to you—your family?"

Saba shook his head, slowly, mournfully. "They didn't make it. My wife Mina and our two beautiful daughters were caught in the market one day by some men who…and when they wouldn't…" His eyes watered.

"Oh God, I'm so sorry Saba."

The old man wiped away his tears. "I escaped that night aboard a boat to Turkey, and then to Greece. It was just me and my youngest child, my only son Joshua. We eventually received asylum to the United States and came here with nothing. I was able to reconnect with a church community that has roots back to my own in Lebanon as Joshua and I learned to heal and move on with our lives. As you can see, I was able to indulge my love of knowledge and turn it into a bookstore. This is my dream…my American dream."

Saba took his glass of wine and drained it. "The story is so old, and yet my heart grows fresh wounds every time I recollect it. Please forgive the tears of an old man."

"Wow," Daniel whispered. His eyes glazed over but then sprang bright ahead of his question. "What about your son? Does he live nearby?"

The old man shook his head. "No, I'm afraid that he is nowhere near. I raised him as faithfully as a single father could and Joshua was as faithful and loving as any son can be to a father. There's no such thing as perfection, but that boy came as close as it could get. He never caused me grief or heartache."

"So you two are close?"

Saba thought about it, finally nodding. "Yes. Close."

"Do you talk often?"

"Not so much anymore. Joshua made some difficult decisions; ones which unfortunately keep us apart for now. But I understood and I supported him completely." Saba's eyes shone as brightly as black jewels reflecting the light. "Please walk me to the door. It is time for me to go home."

Daniel nodded and stood with Saba, who began to clear the table but Daniel held out his hand. "Please let me do this. You have shown me so much kindness already. I can clear the table."

Saba nodded agreement and thanks. There was a knock on the front door and they walked to it. Daniel opened the door and saw Deborah standing there.

"Ready to go handsome?" she said.

Saba smiled. "Indeed my sweet. Thank you for agreeing to drive me home." He turned toward Daniel. "I'll see you in the morning."

Something nagging on Daniel's mind finally crawled to his tongue. "Saba...how can you be so compassionate, so loving in the face of everything you lost?"

Saba placed his hand upon Daniel's shoulder, his black eyes now soft. "It is our ability to love that makes us most like the Creator...but to love in the face of loss and pain makes us more like God than ever. I'll see you tomorrow, my son."

CHAPTER SEVEN

THE SKY IN Seattle was unusually blue and bright with only a few wisps of clouds hanging above the city. Daniel was on his morning walk: first to the post office where he dropped a white envelope into a blue outgoing bin, and then to his regular java stop on the way back to the store. His hands carried a lidded cup that did little to hide the copious steam escaping from around the edges. His gray eyes rolled upward, gazing upon the vast azure infinity punctured by the white pyramid at the top of Smith Tower. A sip of his coffee reminded him to be thankful about the small enjoyments in life, those little pleasures that are all too easily overlooked or of taken advantage, and yet his eyes traveling again to the earth caught upon someone—and something inside him urged to connect. Daniel recognized the young man from the bus, wearing the same ragged coat and hat.

Daniel walked up to where he was sitting upon ground, leaning his back against the rough, reddish façade of Billy Pints' Bar. Daniel sat down next to the man but kept looking forward. "You still have your hat."

The man chuckled but quickly caught up with himself and stopped. "Yeah. Want something?"

"Just to know your name," Dan said and extended his hand, sharing his own name first.

Thinking for the briefest moment, the man smiled and shook the hand. "Dodger. Nice to meet you."

"You haven't seen those punks since the bus, have you?" Dan asked.

Dodger shook his head. "You?"

Nodding, Dan said, "got jumped. Tore me up pretty good too and got away with everything I had—almost everything."

"Ah. So you *do* want something, you want to get even? Catch them?"

"No no," Dan held up his hand, "I just wanted to make sure that you were still all right. That they didn't get to you too."

"Oh. Well, I'll keep my eyes peeled for those scoundrels—I'll let you know if they show up again."

Dodger's awkward use of language caught Daniel off guard and he noticed the surprise on Dan's face so he reached into his coat pocket and pulled out a roughly beaten copy of *Oliver Twist* by Charles Dickens. "I don't get much chance for talking."

"Good book. How many times have you read it?"

Dodger shrugged. "I don't know, zillions probably. It's always been my favorite book, but I don't even need to read it anymore. Memorized it. Can't really read this one anyway because too many pages are missing. Anyway, it's become the story of my life—without the happy ending. I feel like the Artful Dodger, hence my name."

Daniel laughed. "That's funny because growing up my friends called me Pip."

Now Dodger laughed. "*Great Expectations*, that's a great story too but I haven't read it in ages."

Daniel smiled, "neither have I."

The front door of the bar burst open and a man with an apple shaped midsection and spindly legs protruding downwards stepped through and approached them. Daniel immediately recognized Billy Pints but had never spoken directly with him.

"Hey Dodgy, you had lunch yet?" Billy called out.

Dodger shook his head.

"Whose your friend?" Billy said but a spring of recognition spread upon his brow. "Wait a sec—you're Danny. How you been since your beating? Man you looked like shit."

Dan chuckled. "Saba said you helped get me inside the store afterward. Thank you Mr. Pints."

"Peeled you from the pavement myself. Glad to see you're up and about, young man. I got lunch for you too—come on in you both. And call me Billy."

The bar inside was dark with layers of wood paneling half way until leaving the remaining expanse open with rugged singed brick up to a ceiling that was tiled with a tin relief. Dan liked the feeling of the place. It was something between a sports bar and a speakeasy with low lights and a huge flat screen above the mirror behind the concave old wood bar.

"This way boys," Billy called out while leading them through a door into the kitchen, which was stacked with dishes by the sink. Billy shuffled in front of the grill, which had chopped onions steaming on top. He grabbed his metal spatula and wielded it upon the onions like a skilled samurai, chopping and shaping the onions into two lines upon the hot table. "I know how you like it Dodgy. Danny, do you like peppers and mushrooms on your cheese steak sandwich?"

Dan nodded. "That'd be great."

Billy added peppers and mushrooms and then went to the freezer and came back with a couple of thin sliced sandwich steaks, throwing them upon the grilled vegetables. After chopping it all up and adding provolone, he then scooped it into a couple of hoagie rolls and handed them each a plate.

Billy led them to a table nearby where Dodger sat down and tucked into his sandwich. Dan took his tenuous first bite, and was pleased by the result.

Billy took his kitchen towel and slung it over his shoulder before sitting across from Dan. "So how's working for Saba?"

"Good. He's pretty hands off with the project but very supportive."

Billy nodded. "You have no idea. I may own this place, but if it wasn't for Saba it would still be my biggest bitch."

"What do you mean?" Dan said through a mouthful of meat and onions.

Billy rubbed his head of white hair. "You're not the first that the old man has helped. When he found me, I was completely trapped...and I mean in a bottle. I would run this place all night and then crash all day, get up with a bottle of Jack and get going again for the next evening. I've been married twice but divorced twice for the same reason: I couldn't give it up. My wives had to give up on me and I eventually learned to give up on myself. I was convinced that life with a shot glass in your mouth was just the way it was supposed to be for me. Saba knew otherwise. He was the one to help me to Swedish Medical Center when he found me unconscious, in the alley, in a pool of my own vomit. He convinced me that life is worth living outside of the cage I built for myself. I got help. And I got out."

Dan looked around at the bar with wide eyes.

"Ah, so you wonder why I keep the bar?" Billy asked and Dan nodded. "I'll admit that it's been tough, but the truth is that I like serving people—I just can't do it from behind that bar. That's why I have Charlie do it for me. She runs the drinks and I short order cook from back in the kitchen. I might be out of the way, but I know my regulars and they know me."

Dan finished the sandwich and sat back.

"You done with that?" Dodger asked, pointing at the empty plate, and Dan affirmed. Dodger took both plates into the kitchen.

"So what's *his* story?" Dan said, indicating Dodger.

"It's not really mine to tell," Billy said. "But if you ask him yourself, I'm sure you'll be bound to find out. Just mind you that Dodgy doesn't open up too fast, you'll need to earn his trust."

"Has Saba tried to help him?"

"Sure. We all try to help. The only problem is that someone can only be helped if they know they need it. Dodgy's not quite there yet." Billy said.

A crashing sound came from the kitchen and Billy was on his feet quicker than a thrown cat. "What the hell is going on in there Dodgy?"

"I got it under control!" Dodger's voice sounded from the kitchen.

Billy sat down, a wide smile on his wide face. "I'm happy to feed Dodgy for free, but he insists on doing the dishes. He's a good kid, he just needs to help himself. We all do."

Dan scratched his sandpaper like chin. "So how many people has Saba helped?"

Billy shrugged his thick shoulders and arched his brow. "Dunno. But I know there's a lot of folks he's reached out to, just not all of them wanted the help. Saba may be a funny old fart, but he likes his projects and his favorites are broken souls."

"Well there's plenty of those."

"You said it Danny."

CHAPTER EIGHT

DANIEL HURDLED THROUGH the store door. "Saba, I'm back."

"A bit longer than usual," Saba called out from a back corner of the store.

"I'm sorry, it's just that—,"

"You met Billy Pints. Cheese steak sandwiches, I'm guessing." The old man stepped out from the book cases.

Dan stood back, wary. "How did you know?"

Saba held up a knobby brown finger, pointing at Dan's shirt. "I spy a mushroom."

Dan rolled his eyes and peeled the mushroom from his shirt and tossed it into a trash bin. "So what are we working on today?"

"That depends," Saba said, placing his index finger on his chin dimple.

"On what?"

"On how long you visit with your guest." Saba led Dan through the stacks of books back to a sitting nook where a woman with blonde locks about her shoulders sat, staring back at him.

"Bridgette..."

She sat still, her eyes filling with tears but none running down yet.

Saba approached her and knelt to her level. "I believe that you said you like your tea with lemon? Earl Grey?"

Bridgette nodded. Saba stood up and walked back into the book stacks without so much as a glance toward Daniel.

Dan stared at her in confusion and then followed Saba toward the kitchen. "What is she doing here?" He whispered.

"She came to see you, Daniel. Would you like some tea as well?"

"To hell with tea! Why would she come down here?"

Saba turned toward him with a stern face. "It is very rude to keep her waiting longer than she already has been. Bridgette is your guest, so be gracious."

Daniel left the kitchen and walked back to the nook where he unceremoniously dropped into the nearest seat across from Bridgette. "So you found me."

She shrugged her shoulders. "I had to do something."

"Do something about what?"

"You walked out. I don't hear from you or see you for weeks. I even called the police to ask if anything had happened to you. I was worried."

"Well imagine that," Dan said.

Bridgette shook her head, her glimmering blue eyes brimming with moisture. "Yes. And I came to apologize Daniel. Please come home."

Daniel now shook his head and looked her square in the face. "I'm not ready for either of those things. You know why."

"Yes, I know your reasons and the fact that we continue to avoid the subject. Why can't we just talk about this?"

"I don't want to talk about *this*."

Saba strolled through in between them, placing a steaming mug of tea in front of Bridgette and then placed one in front of Daniel.

"How did you find me here?"

Bridgette then looked at Saba. "I let her know you were here, and that you were all right," he said.

Daniel felt a spike of anger flare but then subside, and then he slumped over his tea. Saba left them alone as he retreated among the bookshelves.

"Please don't be mad at him. He was just..."

"Butting into our business." Dan said.

"No, he was helping. I worry about you Daniel. I thought that you would be gone for a day or two at the most, but for over two months?"

Daniel continued to skulk over his tea while her bright blue eyes continued to penetrate his veneer.

"All right Dan, I will leave you alone. Please forgive me—for everything."

"You'll have to keep waiting on that one."

Bridgette stood and shrugged her shoulders. "However it has to be."

Daniel nodded in compliance. He stood and walked her to the front door. Saba also came over from the back and held out his hand. "It was a pleasure to meet you Bridgette. You are as beautiful as a sunny day in Seattle. May you be blessed."

She laughed, filling the space with the light timbre of her voice. "Thank you Saba for your help."

"I'm always here to help," said the old man with a wry grin.

She then turned toward Daniel, who stood with his arms crossed. "Please don't give up. I'll be waiting."

Bridgette walked out the heavy oaken front door which followed her with a resounding bang as it closed shut.

"I'll have to fix that at some point," Dan said.

"I agree," Saba said.

"I was talking about the door."

"I wasn't."

Dan turned to face him. "What is your deal, old man? Why are you trying to help me? And what was that all about—you know, inviting her down here?"

Saba drew deeply and exhaled. "I was married for fifteen wonderful and terrible years. Terrible because of the tragedies we faced. Wonderful because I had someone to share them with. You are only cheating yourself, Daniel."

Dan shook his head and backed away. "I'm not the one cheating. She was. It was an affair with Marcus, her coworker. That's why I'm not going home."

"Ah," Saba said, scratching his bald pate. "I suspected infidelity, but to be honest I'm a bit shocked and twisted around over it being her. I'm assuming it's over with Marcus?"

Daniel nodded.

"And you know that she wants you back?"

"It doesn't matter. The pain won't go away."

"Yes, I do understand something about pain," Saba said. "Do you love her?"

Daniel looked at Saba with hurt eyes.

"Do you love her?"

"Yes," Dan said. "Yes dammit I do love her." He left Saba standing by the front door and retreated back up the stairs to the loft above.

Saba nodded ruefully.

CHAPTER NINE

DAN ATTACHED A final fascia board for the thirteenth bookcase that he had been able to preserve and update. He tried to keep the original cases since they were constructed rather finely of beech and given a dark stain. He stood back and observed his work, his eyes jumping from the old wood to the new and wondering how quickly he could finish the other twenty-one cases so he could stain them all at once. He set down the hammer and stood up, brushing off the work dust from his shirt while he glanced outside and couldn't help but feel a pang of envy for the pedestrians outside spending their afternoons in the sunshine. Seattle had warmed up in the recent weeks, a foreboding tell of a warmer summer to come.

He walked over to the kitchen and poured a glass of iced water from the fridge, downing it in gulps to quench the dryness cracking his throat. Pouring one more glass, Dan stepped back onto the floor of *Olde Mysterium*, taking it in. The new lights were installed and working their magic with the soft glow of warm rays spilling upon the brick walls and bookcases. His eyes traveled over to the next rack he would tackle in his bid to reinforce and update the sales floor, but he saw that it was out of place. It stood ajar from the wall where it had been flush earlier that morning.

Dan approached the bookcase but was able to notice upon closer inspection that this particular rack was unique from the rest. It was also a door. Dan glanced about to see if Saba was present, but the old man had left to run some errands and placed Dan in charge of the shop. Daniel went to the front door and locked it, placing the return clock in the window to alert customers of his return in fifteen minutes time. He approached the secret door as if viewing something illicit and stopped just before the bookcase ajar. Craning his neck, he could see beyond a dimly lit stairwell leading downward and pushed open the secret door enough that he could step through and begin his own descent down into the unknown. His stomach tied into its own knot as he took each nimble step with the grace of a cat.

Dan's eyes adjusted to the low light as he reached the bottom where he saw an old door. With his heart pounding in his ears, Daniel reached out his hand, holding it as steady as it would go, and he turned the doorknob. He was certain he didn't know what he would find, but if it was meant to be hidden then it must be something important. Daniel had always wondered what dark secrets Saba might be hiding and there was a part of himself that didn't want to know, but he turned the knob anyway and pushed open the door.

The space beyond was simple with concrete walls and basic lighting, but there was a desk full of papers in the corner beneath the spotlight of its own stained glass desk lamp. His gray eyes traveled the expanse of the room, capturing all the newspaper clippings and pictures of people in Pioneer Square with sticky notes attached next to them. There was a chalk board with some interesting writing on it that looked like Greek mixed with Arabic, but he had no idea what it said.

Dan walked over to a picture of Jerusalem, his eyes gazing all over the place, trying to decipher what the handwriting on the poster was: some of it English, and some he was sure to be Arabic. Then as he pulled away, he noticed something else hanging prominently in the room...a plaque stating a quote by William Blake, "The truth can never be told so as to be understood and not believed."

He walked closer to the desk, leaning over it to glimpse at the papers but not wanting to touch anything for fear of disrupting the chaos. "What is all of this?" He said under his breath.

"Quite simply my son, this is what I do with my collected knowledge," the old man's voice startled Daniel, throttling his heart into his neck with adrenaline.

"Saba you scared me."

"Well in my defense you were the one investigating my workshop."

Dan threw up his hands. "Sorry, I found the hidden door and then I just had to find out what was down here. What is this?"

Saba held his hands out, waving over everything in the room. "This is just something fun for me to do when I am alone. I have spent a lifetime gathering information, storing it away and trying to make sense of where it all fits in."

"You mean like a puzzle?"

"Exactly like a puzzle! You see Daniel, what may appear to be a random chaos of events forming the mould of our history has been guided and shaped all along the way, bringing us to our current place in time. And what we do now today will affect what will be tomorrow, but not without divine guidance."

"You mean you're talking about destiny? I'm not so sure I agree with you. After all I like to think that I affect my own destiny. What about free will?"

Saba shrugged his shoulders. "Actually I was talking about prophecy. I've spent these last lonely years studying what I believe to be a revelation of well...Revelation, so to speak."

"Saba, I know a little bit about prophecy from my upbringing, but it alone would suggest predestination— and I'm not so sure that everything has been designed for us. I don't want to be a puppet of my own fate, helpless to control the outcome."

The old man chuckled. "I understand your concern, but that's only half of the equation. And to be puppets of fate would be depressing indeed. However there is another way to look at this ages old problem, and it has to do with the faulty assertions laid within the premise of the logic...in other words, the arguments of free will versus predestination are based upon the fact that those two things are mutually exclusive within our own three dimensions of reality, which is true. However the argument itself places God within a box, assuming that he too exists only within the dimensions of our reality. When the truth is simply this: God exists both in our reality and outside of it. He created space and time and matter and can exist outside of his creation yet while existing within it everywhere. In short, God is omnipresent and can be everywhere at once: in the past, our present, and the future, as well as outside and beyond those boundaries."

Dan held up his hands, "okay I'm confused because what it sounds to me like you're saying is that because God can exist inside and outside our world and time, that he can know what we are going to do? Where's the free will in that?"

"The free will exists in us. God may know what we are going to do before we do it, but he will not intervene upon our decisions. We are forced to do nothing by him, despite his foreknowledge of our actions...either for good or bad. That is where the free will comes into play."

Dan sighed. "So what you are saying is that when it comes to free will versus destiny the answer is...?"

"Yes."

"Yes?"

Saba nodded.

"Okay so tell me. How does prophecy fit in with all of this? If collecting knowledge was a means to an end in studying prophecy, then how can you predict the future? Prophecy is all about the future...isn't it?"

The old man held up his pointer finger. "It is and yet it isn't. I believe that God created his prophecies as a way to demonstrate his faithfulness. He tells us what he's going to do, then he fulfills it in our midst without us even knowing it. Only then does he turn us around to look at the spectrum of history and show us his handiwork and the keeping of his promises. It's a lot like our daily living. We experience pain, suffering, oppression and yet God can always find a way to turn pain into love. Only then does he turn us around to show us his handiwork."

"I'm not so sure I follow," Dan said.

"The point is that this is an exercise of the mind. A simple way for an old man to bide his time in between the lonely hours. I need to clarify that this is only my hobby. My occupation is something far more interesting and important than trying to figure out dusty old prophecies."

"What's that?" Dan asked.

Saba smiled and placed his hand on Dan's shoulder. "You my son. Now let's go and open the shop."

CHAPTER TEN

IT ALL BEGAN with a simple phone call. Dan initiated the process, deciding that the time was ripe to call his wife. They shared a couple of congenial conversations on the phone, friendly and nice but not excessively deep, and all with one silent understanding: Bridgette would not push Daniel into returning home and he would not bring up her affair.

Every time Dan would go to sleep in the loft, he would look at the fractured frame of their wedding photo and after a while he began to recognize the feeling in his gut, wondering if he and Bridgette could fix their fractured marriage. Then it rose upon him one morning when Dan realized that he actually wanted to begin finding ways to repair their relationship. He was tired of finding fault in himself or in her. So he called her.

Dan let Bridgette pick the place of their meeting, and she had the good sense to pick the Starbucks nearby. He walked through the door and could see immediately that she secured the best corner table in the place, next to a window for people watching but also the most private spot in the joint. As he approached, his eyes spied two steaming mugs upon the table. He sat opposite and gave her his warmest grin.

"I ordered for you," she said in her soft voice.

"Thanks."

Bridgette took a sip of her coffee. "You look different."

He gave her a look as if to say: *how?*

Her blue eyes wandered over him, examining Daniel from his ears to his fingertips. "I'm not sure how. Everything appears the same, but..."

Dan smiled. "I know what you mean. I've changed in some ways, but it's hard to measure."

"That's it. In all the years I've known you I've never seen you at peace with yourself. You look more confident...and happy."

Now his gray eyes brushed over her and he could see something different as well, but it was heavy almost as if a burden slumped her shoulders downward. "How are you doing?"

Her blonde curls bobbed as she nodded. "Fine. Work's been busy, which is good because I am able to keep focused on the things that are important...you are important Daniel."

"I know you keep saying that, but I need to heal these wounds before we can ever consider moving forward."

"I understand," she said and then took a sip.

Dan ran his fingers through his hair. "Look, I've been so pissed off that I haven't been able to cool to a point where I could think straight. But somehow working at *Olde Mysterium* has allowed me to find something amazing...to find myself. And now I'm beginning to treat these open sores on my soul. The point is this: I woke up the other morning and realized how much I miss waking up next to you."

Bridgette's blue eyes glistened. A single tear ejected from it's duct and ran down her blushed cheek. "Wow. I didn't expect to hear that."

"So there it is," Dan said, holding up his hands. "There's just one thing. I can tell you are keeping something from me. And if you can't tell me what it is...then we have no point in moving forward. There must be complete honesty in order for us to work. We are only as sick as the secrets we keep."

The tears now ran freely down her face; the trails gleaming in the soft light of the coffee house. "What do you want to know?"

He sighed. "Whatever it is that you are keeping from me." Dan had yet to touch the mug before him. "Are you still seeing him?"

She shook her head.

"When was the last time you saw him?"

Her eyes glanced away before returning to focus on the piercing stare of his gray eyes. "Three nights ago."

Dan sat back in his chair. "I thought you were serious about us getting back together."

"I am." Her eyes now bright and wide. Her shoulders were drawn into a defensive posture.

"Then why..." he stopped. Dan didn't know what to say next, so he toyed with his mug. "Then why were you still seeing him? All the while you were still talking to me. Were you keeping your options open?"

"No. I broke it off. I've been trying to break it off for months now, but he won't let go."

Dan appraised his wife for a long while, trying to figure out what it was he was seeing in her but it was obvious after a few moments: shame. "And it's difficult for you to break it off when you are feeling alone all the time?"

Bridgette's tears began afresh as she nodded, unable to speak.

"This is your mess to fix honey. I'm trying to feel sorry for you right now, but I don't." Dan stood up. "Stop keeping your options open." He turned and walked straight through the coffee house and out the front door without so much as a glance backward.

CHAPTER ELEVEN

UPON GETTING BACK to the store, Dan walked passed Saba in a storm of emotion and was about to go up the stairs to his loft when he halted to the sound of a familiar voice.

"Daniel? Is that you?"

Dan stopped and turned. A customer in the store surprised him. It didn't take long for Dan to realize it was one of his old buddies from the Seattle P.I. "Brad?"

Brad ran up and gave Dan a hug. "Oh man, what are you doing here? And I mean what are you doing *here*?"

"This–is where I work," Dan said with a shrug.

Brad glanced around. "Interesting. I would've thought you to be somewhere in California working for another paper. Man you were *on fire* at the P.I., what happened?"

Dan gave a half smile. "Life."

"Wow."

"How about you? What have you been up to?" Dan said to change the subject.

"Been doing okay. The Post-Intelligencer hasn't been the same without you, but the P.I. on the web continues to be an interesting experiment...sometimes resulting in futility. Advertising revenue for a news website can be difficult to find and yet the overhead is lower so there's a larger room of error to work with. You know how it goes. Are you still writing? The last time I saw you, you were talking about that book you were working on. How's that going?"

Dan shuffled. He couldn't help but notice Saba pass through the stacks on the other side, obviously listening in on their conversation. "Uh, to be honest I haven't had time to write lately. Maybe I'll get back to it someday."

"You bet. I know how that goes. How's Bridgette?"

"Fine," Dan said in his most confident tone, but he knew his body language gave him away. Brad was an expert at sniffing out the news.

"Dan, what's going on?"

"Nothing," he said and looked away. Dan knew he was a terrible liar; it was one of the things that he prided himself on...except right then. "Bridgette and I are split. I live above this store and work here fixing up the place."

Brad gave a thin whistle. "I'm sorry to hear that man. So...how are things going here?"

Dan nodded. "Better than I expected."

"Good for you," Brad gave Dan a playful slap on the shoulder. Now Daniel recognized that Brad was lying poorly. Brad looked at his watch. "It's been great to catch up with you man, but I've gotta jet. I just popped in here for a sec while Hillary shops next door." Hillary was Brad's assistant, and Dan wondered if Brad's wife knew about their special friendship yet. Everyone at the office knew about Brad's philandering, and yet somehow it had never erupted in his face. In fact Daniel was now wondering how it could be that an arrogant shite like Brad could get away with so much...and above it all he still had his job at the P.I.

Brad pulled a business card out of his jacket and handed it to Daniel. "Look me up next week. I can find you a story or two to cover, if you're interested. After all we go way back."

Yes, Daniel thought, *way back*. With a numb smile on his face, Daniel reached out and took the business card.

Brad flashed him a wide, white grin and then opened the solid front door. *Bing.* The store bell rang as he walked out into the crisp sunshine.

Daniel's sense of cosmic injustice flooded his brain and pounding shots of hot blood rushed into his face. The anger boiled beneath the surface but he dared not let it out, for Daniel could not know what to expect from himself. His gray eyes glanced down at the card in his hand and then he stepped toward the front window, watching Brad give perky, happy, ditzy Hillary a kiss before stopping in front of a Porsche parked curbside. The yellow paint of the car's body shone bright, as if aglow in the sunlight. It was a new car. He knew Brad's previous vehicle to be an older but well-kept BMW. Now the bastard had spanking-new, racing-yellow Porsche.

The blood in Dan's face pounded even harder as he saw Brad open the passenger door for his mistress-assistant and then hop in himself and speed away. To be pissed-off could not even begin to describe the depth of Daniel's rage.

"That's a nice car," spoke a familiar voice.

Dan startled out of his thoughts to see Saba standing next to him, watching the whole scene unfold. The old man turned to Daniel with his wizened black eyes which were full of compassion.

Daniel tore up Brad's business card and threw it upon the ground. With an expletive, he threw open the front door. *Bing.* And walked out.

CHAPTER TWELVE

The remainder of the afternoon had been a hazy blur of anger. Daniel arrived at Volunteer Park where he found himself pondering the fruitlessness of his daily existence while looking at Noguchi's Black Sun, a black granite sculpture resembling something of a carved charcoal doughnut. The hole in the middle of the sculpture housed enough space to perfectly frame a view of the Space Needle. Threading the needle. Dan had always been uncomfortable looking at this big, black sun with a hole in the center, but at that very moment he felt more at home with the Black Sun than he did anywhere else. What a befitting commentary this artwork spoke into Daniel's life because for the first time he could actually identify with the Black Sun, and the hole in the center of his own soul.

His gray eyes drifted away from the black sun over upon the grass nearby where a young couple laid upon a blanket, kissing. Daniel's heart constricted and he stood up, walking away, meandering without aim toward a great glass greenhouse—the conservatory. He passed through the translucent front doors and meandered, trying to admire the dazzling spray of color contained within the tropical foliage and yet these amazing specimens of nature could not distract him from the growing pain within. He appeared to be the only one there and yet he felt not alone. His gaze raked through the conservatory, over and through the leafy green but he could not detect another person there. Daniel let his feet lead him forward until he turned a corner, witnessing something profoundly and innocently hurtful. An older couple, both with heads of shining white hair sat upon a bench, absorbing the natural works of living art and holding hands. Neither said anything to the other but they seemed confident and comfortable in their silence as if they had shared two lifetimes together and needed not to speak because their thoughts had become one. Their brittle, bony hands were clasped in a loose grasp and yet seemed immovable from each other.

Daniel felt frustrated at not being alone; frustrated that he could not find a space public enough to drown in his own self loathing without the reproachful reminder of life's happinesses. His miserable heart burned and he could no longer stay there. Daniel's gut reacted in a need for something more visceral—craving a vice to shout over the din of his internal despair. He paced out and away from the conservatory and over to the nearest curbside bus stop, where a large metro bus seemed awaiting him for this very escape.

Aboard the bus, Daniel found a certain amount of anonymity as he plopped down into the nearest seat toward the front. His eyes had scanned the handful of passengers and found only dour looks and sour pouts. He was finally in the right place.

The bus sped away and headed south out of the Capitol Hill neighborhood, turning right on Madison and continuing it's journey into the heart of downtown Seattle. Daniel felt himself being pulled back toward Pioneer Square and *Olde Mysterium*, but he railed against the prospect. He was not in any way ready to head back to the scene of his current predicament. Then he spied a place where he realized he could get away to escape from his turmoil, if only for a couple of hours anyway. Daniel reached up and pulled on the stop cord. A bell rang up front by the driver and the bus pulled again to the curbside.

As he stepped off the bus Daniel realized that what had been a lovely sunny day had now turned sour upon itself and began to spit out rain. He felt the comfort of the drops on his shoulders and head as he marched forward toward an establishment he had always seen but never entered. The small moral warning in the back of his mind was squelched by the overdriving need to escape, to lick his wounds, and to forget about Bridgette and her lover as well as Brad and his mistress, and his yellow new sports car, and his damned job.

In complete and justified defiance, Daniel opened the door to one of the most well known and windowless establishments in Seattle: Déjà Vu.

Several seconds passed before Daniel's eyes adjusted to the dim lighting inside and he had no idea what to expect since he had never been inside Déjà Vu before— or any other strip club for that matter, but he figured there's a first time for everything. The coat check waved him through, explaining that there was no cover charge in the afternoon. Daniel reached into his pocket and felt for the thick wad of bills there; it was money he had planned to give to Bridgette at their meeting, but that changed.

The main room stood wide and pink and purple lights shone from floor to ceiling, which was tiled in black and dark gray. Music boomed from speakers overhead, thumping a sleazy Euro dance beat accompanied by a sexy saxophone. Daniel found a rather sizable scattering of watchers, sitting mostly at their own tables, and all with their eyes fixed up front. His eyes followed their direction to the stage and witnessed the sensuous sight of a lithe female figure spinning about on a silver pole with the ease of a gymnast. The shock of pink hair on her head was not the only thing that appeared fake, and yet Daniel could not look away.

"Hey there Skipper, are you going to sit and order something?" a strong female voice next to him spoke.

Daniel shook his head loose from the enchantment. "Yeah sure." He let the waitress lead the way while he looked again at the stage. She stopped next to an empty table and he sat.

"So what'll it be?"

"Ummm, how about three fingers of Scotch?"

She chuckled and he turned his head to look at her, where he noticed for the first time that she wore a tight black vest with a plunging neck line and a skirt that covered almost nothing. The blood rushed to his head but he worked overtime to keep his cool. "What's so funny?"

"You're a newbie. Never been to a strip club in Seattle before?" Her white smile seemed genuine and friendly and her eyes seemed almost compassionate, as if watching him lose his virginity on the spot.

Daniel shook his head.

"The city doesn't allow alcohol in the clubs...so how about a Coke?"

"Sure," Dan said, embarrassment creeping all over him. How could he have known? He tried to let it roll off his back, but instead the discomfort stuck snugly between his shoulder blades. He was trying to disappear, but he knew he stood out like a coal out of the fire.

"It's okay sweetie. I don't get to see newbies everyday. Most of the men here are regulars and they know how to spend their money, but I got a good feeling about you." She winked and pointed to her name badge. "My name's Trixie and I'll be right back with your Coke. Okay?"

Dan nodded and Trixie disappeared to the bar where a burly man in a black shirt with a watchful eye poured soft drinks. Dan noticed that he wasn't watching the dancer, but his eyes roamed the room over the heads of the crowd and then stopped with a hard stare on

Daniel. He averted his gaze to the stage where the dancer whipped her pink hair about and then flipped around on the pole and held her body upside down while her legs lasciviously split into a single long line, forming herself into a perfect letter *T.* The crowd of men clapped and cheered as she held herself there, showing off her strength while exposing every crevice of her body to the hungry eyes in the room.

"Cinnamon's on fire this afternoon," Trixie said as she placed the Coke in front of Daniel, her nod motioning to the dancer upfront now working an angle that seemed reminiscent of a contortionist.

Daniel's eyes looked away and found his drink in front of him. He sipped it in silence when he saw Trixie sit down across from him. "You need to pay for that."

"Oh, right," Dan reached in and pulled out a twenty dollar bill. "I don't know how much these cost but..."

"That'll do just fine," Trixie said and took the twenty, putting it in her vest pocket.

Dan shrugged his shoulders and looked down again at his drink.

"Okay Skipper, what's wrong?"

Dan sipped his drink. "I'm just...having one shitty day."

Trixie leaned forward over the table, as if seeking a better read on Dan's face. "And so you came here to let it all go did'ya?"

"Something like that."

"It's all right honey. Everybody here is trying to escape something. Even Cinnamon up there."

Dan's eyes glanced briefly to Cinnamon's body flipping all around the pole, but then trained them back on Trixie. Her eyes had a lovely almond shape. "Even you?"

Now she smiled with straight, white teeth behind her sultry colored lips. "Especially me. We're all survivors here Skipper, so welcome to the club."

Daniel's eyes traveled with Trixie's shapely form as she returned to the bar. A change in music brought his eyes back to the stage where he noticed that a new performer emerged and Cinnamon disappeared. The new dancer had bright blonde hair, but it wasn't nearly as shocking. He sipped his Coke in silence as his eyes drank in the new performance, which was more rhythmic and dance-based than Cinnamon's gymnastics. Glancing around at the other patrons, he could see the other waitresses were also flirting with their customers and walking away with plenty of money to show for it.

"Hey there," spoke a sultry voice.

Dan turned to see Cinnamon joining him at his table. Her pink hair was now draped over her shoulders and the rest of her was barely covered in black lace. His expression felt frozen in surprise but if she noticed, she had the good form to not show it.

"Trixie tells me you're new."

Dan nodded and tipped his glass for another sip but it was empty.

"That's cool. I like new guys. If you like I can show you around."

Dan looked again around the place; there didn't seem like much more to show.

Cinnamon laughed. Her voice was smoky-sexy. "No silly. You are so cute. What I meant was that I can take you into the back room and dance for you...personally?"

A rush of blood filled into his brain and then filtered away just as quickly to other areas in demand, leaving him lightheaded and embarrassed. He shook his head. "No-no thank you. Maybe..."

"Rain check?" Cinnamon said and flashed one of the most attractive smiles Dan had ever seen. "I'll hold you to it." She stood up and sauntered the room before being waved over by another customer.

"She didn't offer you a dance?" Trixie said, standing over him with her drink plate in her hand.

"No, she did. It's just that I...I mean I'm..."

"I get it," she said with a knowing grin.

"Sorry, I didn't mean to let her down."

"Skipper you didn't let anyone down. Cinnamon'll make a lot of money off these guys." Trixie said and then set her tray with one drink on the table and sat down again across from Dan. "So what are you trying to escape anyway?"

"To be honest, I'm still trying to figure it out myself," Dan said and then placed his head in his hands. This experience had not quite become what he had hoped for. Instead of getting away from his griefs, they seemed to be teeming around him, mocking him.

"It's okay. I like you Skipper. We can talk about it later...if you want to." Trixie placed another Coke in front of him. "This one's on me."

Dan raised his head enough to see Trixie walk away again, and he still couldn't help admiring her as she went but he couldn't focus for long because his core tugged at something deep inside. Yet there was no way to figure out what it was, at least not yet. He lifted the glass up and took in a long draught of the soda. His eyes caught sight of something before setting his glass down, something written on his napkin:

off @ 10

trixie 555-1820

He looked again at Trixie serving another customer. She glanced his direction with a smirk. Dan's heart pounded in his chest, heating him up from the inside all the more. It had been a long time since any woman showed a true interest in him and he didn't know quite what to make of it.

"She's very attractive don't you think?"

"Jesus Christ!" Dan spun in his chair to see Saba sitting next to him.

"No, I'm talking about Trixie." The old man pointed in her direction.

"What are you doing here?" Dan said.

"I have a few friends here," Saba said just as Cinnamon waved at the old man. Saba then nodded at the burly bartender, who smiled and nodded in return. "Tank at the bar told me you've been jumpy since you came in. It made him nervous but I told him that you were all right and that you're a friend of mine."

Dan's mouth hung open and his eyes stood wide in shock.

Saba gave him a genuine but knowing smile. "What are you doing here Daniel?"

"I'm not sure how to answer that. I don't even really know."

The old man nodded. "Sometimes there are no simple answers for difficult decisions no matter how misguided. However I am not bereft of insight for something like this."

Daniel raised an eyebrow.

"It is not uncommon for pain and pleasure to be strange bedfellows."

"Pardon?"

"You heard correctly," Saba said and motioned around. "This place is an excellent example. It's an entire business built upon allowing men to trade the pain in their ordinary lives for a few hours of pleasure—at the cost of a pretty penny."

"So what do the women get out of it?"

"Easy money, a false sense of security, and a taste of control. However, every woman here is here for need—be it particular or myriad."

"I'm not sure I follow you," Dan said, sipping his Coke.

Saba held up one knobby finger and pointed toward a giggling Cinnamon leading a customer away toward the back room. "Heidi is her real name. As a little girl she wanted to be a ballerina, and she has the grace and body control to prove it possible."

"So what happened?" Dan said.

"She was raised by a single father who was a mean drunk. She grew up belittled and terrified...and abused. Fear of men became a regular theme in her life because

she knew none that were kind but her regular escape
was funneled through dancing. Once she hit high school
and filled out, she discovered the amount of control she
could have over other men and honed that skill to a
razor's edge. However when she got pregnant by one of
the boys, he left her and she dropped out of school to
leave her home so that her father wouldn't abuse her
little girl too. She was briefly homeless before coming
here. Now she makes enough to keep a roof over her
and her daughter's heads."

"So you're saying that her being here is okay?"

"Not at all! I'm simply showing that she is trapped.
She has no diploma, no real job experience, and this
career path has a very young expiration date unless she
moves on to worse things."

Dan shrugged his shoulders. "Okay so that's
Cinnamon—er Heidi."

Saba smiled, recognizing a challenge and so he
indicated Tank behind the bar. "Tank is from Iowa and
came from a family with a controlling father and an
absent mother. His one redeeming talent seemed to be
in sports, or so he thought. It was the only thing his
father supported him in. He eventually got a football
scholarship to the University of Washington but lost it
in his sophomore year due to drug testing: steroids. He's
been working here as a bartender and bouncer for the

last year and he hasn't had the courage to tell his family yet that he quit school."

"What about Trixie?"

"Sandy's her name. She was married for five years before ending in a messy divorce. Her ex-husband has sole custody of her son and won't let her visit due to her increasingly violent temper brought on by alcoholism. She moved to Seattle from Portland for a fresh start and began waitressing at Denny's. One night late, after Déjà Vu closed, a couple of dancers came in to the restaurant and she found out how much more she could earn by waitressing here instead. She is a boiling cauldron of rage, and I haven't quite figured out how to get to her yet."

Dan exhaled and slid the napkin with her number on it across the table. "Be my guest."

"Ah! Thank you, this will do nicely." Saba tucked the napkin into his shirt pocket.

"Okay so how do you know all of this? Do you come here frequently?"

"Not as much as I should, but I'm glad you came here because it reminded me of how much I miss these people."

"What made you come in here to begin with?"

"The same as you, but this is where I found Deborah working. She reminded me of my daughter and I found out that she was working to put herself through school. We became friends and I helped her find a better way."

Dan shook his head and rubbed his eyes. "You're a hard one to understand old man."

Saba shrugged and smiled.

Cinnamon then waltzed over and sat at their table. "Hey Saba, why don't you come around much anymore? It's good to see you." She kissed him on the cheek.

"I'm sorry lovely, but you're never far from my mind."

"Would you like to go in the back?"

"There is nothing I could possibly want more at this moment. Would it be all right if Dan joined us?"

Dan shook his head and held up his hands in protest but he was undone by Cinnamon. "Don't you say 'no' to me silly. I insist." With that she took his hand and led both men into the secluded back room.

The V.I.P. lounge, had bright pink walls muted by the low lighting. The tiling on the floor was arranged in a black and gray checkerboard, and caused Dan to wonder how much and what kind of sweat and other filth he was walking over. Cinnamon led Saba to a chair positioned against a pole in the center of the room, where she held his hand while he sat down. She then plucked up another chair from a stack in the corner and sat it down next to the old man but motioned for Dan to sit in it. Reluctantly he obeyed. He noticed the music in this room was different, smoother than the electro thumping in the main room. Dan was curious but cautious what was going to happen.

"First things first my dear?" Saba said in a cool tone.

"Whatever you prefer, but you don't have to," she replied.

Saba reached into his khaki jacket and pulled out a thick wad of bills, handing the stack over to Cinnamon, who shook her head. "No no that's too much and you know it."

The old man pushed the bills into her hand. "Think of it as a back payment on the time we should have spent together."

Tears welled up in her eyes and she used a cautious finger to wipe them away. "You have always been far too kind to me...more than I deserve."

"That's rubbish and you know it," Saba gleamed. "You are so valuable Heidi, and someday you will see it too." The old man's smile showed that he wanted badly to hug her, but he left his hands by his side. Dan considered everything to be strange, as if the stripping world had been turned on its ear by one wispy old man. "What are you waiting for? Join us," Saba said.

Cinnamon went over to the corner and turned down the sexy music, then took a chair and set it in front of Saba and Dan, forming a triangle. She sat and looked at both men. "It's been so long. So where do we start?"

Saba grinned even wider. "With you of course. How's little Pearl doing in school?"

"Oh she's so smart, much smarter than I ever was in school. She's practically a straight A student. In fact I don't know how much longer I can keep from her what my job is."

"So you haven't told her yet? She's going into fourth grade isn't she?"

Cinnamon nodded. "I should consider myself fortunate. Every now and then one of her classmate's fathers come in here, but they don't seem to recognize me through the makeup and hair." With this statement she pulled off the shocking pink wig to expose a short, brown bob underneath.

"Your costume is marvelous my dear, and yes you are lucky. Have you considered leaving here? You could be so much more on the outside and your gifts could shine."

She shrugged her shoulders. "I don't have a proper education. What would I do? Where would I go?"

"Now that's not fair. You know I've made you an offer which still stands. I'm ready to help you whenever you are ready to accept it," Saba now reached out and took her hands.

She pulled away. "I can't."

Saba's black eyes were now moist with concern. "Are you still struggling with the other things?"

Cinnamon nodded. "You know I am. It's simply a part of being here and doing what I do. That stuff is just a part of this scene and even though I'm trying hard to kick it, sometimes I find myself needing it just to get through the next dance or the next customer. Last week was really rough."

"How so?" Saba asked but Dan realized that he probably already knew the answer.

"Rent was due and we were almost out of food. Pearl needs school supplies. So I had to do some things that I've never done before." Her tears now flowed freely. "Oh God I'm so ashamed. I'm so filthy."

Saba now reached out and hugged her, cradling her head as if she were his little girl and allowed her to sob into his shoulder. "You are a valuable creation Heidi. And you are beautiful and strong–a survivor. Pearl knows this about you as do I. But she is going to need you more and more as she is at the cusp of her teen years. And she needs you to be a bright and shining star of an example. You can't keep this part of your life a secret from her forever. Pearl will eventually find out, and unfortunately she may end up on this path too if you don't change where you're going."

"I know," Cinnamon choked out as she continued to cry.

Dan's eyes watered, not with sorrow but with clarity and his tears washed away the film of fantasy from this place. For the first time he could see what all of this was—a thinly veiled house of sorrows draped with the promise of pleasure. The woman sitting in front of him being held by Saba had her own demons to deal with, but how could he not have seen it before? Her struggles were just as great if not more than his and yet only earlier he had used her to escape his own problems, ogling her body as a sexual machine but never attaching it to a person with feelings. Heidi had struggles financially, physically, emotionally—and spiritually. Why couldn't she accept Saba's help when it was so clearly in front of her grasp? Why is she so afraid to leave this place? What does she have to lose? As all of these questions swirled within Dan's head, he began to recognize the commonality he shared with Heidi: they were both at the bottom, in the pit where day can be as dark as night. The uncommon love of Saba's actions now dawned on him anew, spreading light on things he had not seen before. Here was the old man offering a new life of meaning for Heidi and her daughter and all she had to do was say *yes* and be willing to walk away from this shitty existence, yet she couldn't pull herself together to do it. But was Daniel similar at all? In the trenches of his soul, he knew where he had been fighting and now he could see for the first time what he was fighting against: fear of change. Yet the difference between him and Heidi was that a certain amount of the choice had been made for him, or so he felt.

Daniel finally realized the great fortune bestowed upon him that began with meeting Saba just before his mugging and beating. Through what appeared to be an unfortunate circumstance, he had been brought into the heart and home of the one man who offered him help and hope. Dan's eyes glanced over Saba, who was soothing Heidi and giving her words of comfort. *This man has made me his son*, he thought, *and he has been a better father to me than my own.* Daniel knew at this exact moment that there was no longer the struggle between his head and heart. He would forever be indebted and loyal to the old man—almost loving him like a father.

CHAPTER THIRTEEN

THE MORNING BEGAN like most; the clouds hanging above the city threatening rain. Dan awoke and clambered down the creaky stairs into the store below. The familiar, comforting smells of coffee and bagels hovered in his face as he made his way back to the kitchen and found Saba pouring the black nectar into each man's mug.

Saba handed him his mug. "Good morning, my son."

"Morning to you too Saba."

Dan took one of the fresh baked bagels and followed Saba onto the store floor, where they both surveyed the room. Dan raked his eyes upon the minor defects of his work, the things he wished he would have done differently but would have to leave it be or find another time altogether to correct. He looked over at Saba and saw him smiling and nodding while his gaze shifted from corner to corner and from wall to wall.

"Your work is very fine and appreciated Daniel," Saba said. "I especially like the restoration of the old murals on the brick."

Daniel liked them too. As he had been tearing away the wall he discovered a couple of old advertisement murals that had been painted on the brick but were badly faded from wear. He took it upon himself to restore the murals to a visible recognition but left them at a point of distress to enhance the old feeling of the bookstore.

"So would you like to know where I'm starting today?" Dan said.

"I already know what we are going to do today. I need you to help me with a personal errand. Are you willing?" Saba said.

Dan nodded. "Sure, what are we doing?"

"I need you to accompany me to my church. There is something today that I must attend, you'll drive us in my car."

Dan felt the apprehension pile up in his stomach but relented. "Sure, when do we go?"

"In ten minutes."

The drive lasted over half of an hour as the rain that had been threatened arrived early and sprayed the windshield of Saba's powder blue GTO. Dan noticed before getting into the car that the exterior was in need of some love but as he started the engine and heard it roar to life, he knew the engine block had been well maintained. Despite the pansy color it would definitely be a classic car to own.

"Up here take a left and the church will be on your right," Saba instructed.

Daniel pulled into a well known Catholic church in north Seattle. "Saba, if your church is—what is it called again?"

The old man smiled. "Melkite."

"Yes. Melkite. Why do you meet at a Catholic church?"

Saba nodded. "Our Melkite mission is the first plant for this area and was designated to reach the needs of the Middle Eastern Christian refugees in Seattle. We desire to have our own building someday, but for now using St. Michael's will do. As for meeting at a Catholic church, our church has roots older than that of the Catholics, but through certain twists of church history, we came under the umbrella of the Vatican and are in communion with them."

"So you're Catholic?"

"Technically yes," Saba laughed. "But the Vatican allows us to maintain our own leadership and keep our rites. We are rather fond of them after all."

Dan nodded as if he understood but was able to hide his slight confusion by focusing on finding a parking space. He helped Saba out of the car and they walked through the front doors of the church and into the sanctuary. Dan felt the hair stand on end along his spine; he had not stepped foot in a church for well over a decade, and he had never been in a Catholic one...much less Melkite. There were people everywhere, dressed in their Sunday best on a Thursday morning. Meandering, talking in low voices.

The sanctuary was not what he imagined. Wood paneling lined the walls, giving out a classic but comfortable feeling. Not much existed in the way of adornment except for a long stained glass window exploding with color in every direction. A simple white cross was outlined in the center of the colorful panes, all of which hung above the apse. Ancient pews ribbed the nave all the way to the front and Dan's eyes traveled up to the two-step raised apse at the end of the church. A basic wooden table served as the altar and he noticed two large golden frames set upon easels, each encompassing the picture of a saint. Long, thin noses.

Smooth facial lines. Round eyes. Heads set inside golden painted halos. Each saint depicted in the iconic style of eastern orthodox religious art. Daniel knew them to be generally called icons.

His apprehension rose with the unfamiliar feeling of the sanctuary, but Dan took his cues of social etiquette from Saba and followed him down the central aisle of the nave and into one of the massive pews. As Dan settled, it was then he noticed the most important object in the room: a coffin. The box sat closed at the base of the apse and had been partially hidden by the front pews, but he now noticed it. In fact he couldn't move his eyes away.

"You didn't tell me we were going to a funeral," Dan whispered.

"Mmmm?" Saba replied, apparently broken from a reverie of his own.

"Who's in *there*?"

Saba placed a finger to his lips, indicating silence.

A long bearded man in full white robes appeared on the apse, his red stole emblazoned with the ornate golden embroidery of a cross and a few other cryptic signs. Daniel had no idea what to make of them. This priest began to cantor the prayers in a crisp, deep voice, and the songs carried the wavering tone and melodic style of the Middle East. The language was completely unrecognizable but Daniel could only assume it to be Arabic. Every now and again, the surrounding parishioners would sing responses in unison at breaking intervals of the prayers. Saba followed along, not sparing Daniel any indication of his confusion or explanation for what was going on. The priest lit candles, waving them before the crowd and then turning to do so before each of the pictured icons before setting them on the altar. Daniel's attention stood rapt. Growing up Baptist, he never knew any church could be so mysterious, cryptic and beautiful. The deep traditions of the people in this place haunted his curiosity. His eyes wandered over the crowd, noticing most of them sharing the swarthy complexion of Saba. He wondered how many people in the church had similar stories of persecution and escape. Yet here they were singing, praying, many of them crying, but doing so together with a bond stronger than any Daniel had ever known.

After the service, Daniel and Saba followed the crowd through the doors, but only after Saba spoke with many of them. Dan was at a loss for any of the conversation since all of it was in Arabic, except for the portions where Saba introduced him and he was greeted with hearty handshakes.

Once inside the powder blue car, Dan turned to Saba. "You didn't tell me it was a *funeral* we were attending today!"

"My apologies, my son. I thought that I had told you, but perhaps it slipped my mind. I haven't been feeling like myself lately."

Daniel exhaled. He could see the swollen bags under Saba's eyes. The old man looked tired and worn, not his usual energetic self. "Is everything all right?"

"Yes, everthing's fine. I'm just trying to catch up."

"Saba, who was in that coffin?"

Saba's black eyes traveled out the side window. "A brave young man who gave everything for his country. He will be missed deeply by his family and his church."

"How terrible. His family must be torn up. Where was he stationed?" Dan said.

"Afghanistan," Saba said, pointing out the window. "Let's follow the funeral procession to the cemetery."

Daniel wheeled over into the line of cars pulling away from the parking lot and following each other. A police escort gave chase in the lead and brought up the rear of the procession. He casually glanced over at his old friend, who continued to watch the passing scenery in silence with his knuckles against his lips in a pensive posture.

The uncomfortable silence of their drive put Daniel on edge. He had always hated funerals and cemeteries. His mind flipped back to his father's funeral, where he felt numb but not without loss and yet Dan's grief stemmed not from losing his father but rather from losing any possibility of the relationship he desired to have with that man. Yet his father had been cold, stubborn, judgmental, and solitary up to the day of his death. The familiar but unwanted feelings weighed heavy in his gut and kept coming like bile. Bridgette had tried to comfort him, but those memories burned worse than acid and so he pushed them away. Dan had to do something; say something. "How terrible."

Saba's ears perked up and he turned his head. "Yes?"

"I was just thinking how terrible and pointless this all is."

"How pointless *what* is?"

Dan breathed deep. "This war. War in general. So many lives lost and so many unnecessary deaths."

"Unnecessary?" Saba said.

"Yeah, like why are we still fighting with these people all the way across the globe? Afghanistan is on the other side of the damn planet!" Daniel caught his zeal and sighed. "Sorry."

"There's nothing to apologize for," Saba said. "But I am curious about your position. Are you saying that death is unnecessary...or is it sacrifice?"

"I mean that death is inevitable, but it shouldn't need to come before it is due. Yes, sacrifice is unnecessary...war is unnecessary. Don't you ever get tired of seeing the bodies of soldiers, women and children on the television? It's a freaking epidemic."

"Yes, in fact that is much of the reason I don't watch the television. There is seldom anything reputable on the screen." Saba said. "But if you don't mind me saying...I disagree with you Daniel."

Daniel's head swiveled on his neck and he stared at the old man, who was looking not only sad, but his journalist gut told him that Saba was crazy. "What?"

"I disagree with your premise." Saba's eyes wandered over and out the window again. "Death comes to us all, that is simply a statement of fact, but not all of us can choose our death. Yet there are those special breed of people who can and do choose not only to face death, but do so with brevity of purpose...those brave few who stand guard ready to do battle in order to protect us."

Dan shook his head. "Saba, come on. I mean even the war in Iraq was illegal, and the operations in Afghanistan and Pakistan are questionable *at best*. There has been no declaration of war by the Congress."

"Our current conflicts are not illegal. The United States has been engaged in hundreds of conflicts since its founding, both domestic and abroad. Yet a declaration of war has only happened five times."

Dan's eyes opened in disbelief.

Saba gave a grim smile. "It's true. Not only that, but our current struggles are not the first encounter the United States has had with Islamic peoples. The first were the Barbary Wars under the direction of Thomas Jefferson...neither of which were declared by Congress. It was fully understood the President had unquestioned authority to use martial force and subdue the North African pirates. It's all a far cry from where we are today."

Daniel's mouth opened and then closed, but then he said, "why haven't I heard of these things before? I mean I'm a journalist for God's sake...or at least I was one. This stuff was never taught to me in school."

"That's understandable, since it is becoming more difficult to teach the truth especially to our young. The current environment of education isn't conducive to truth telling. But just in case you are still in doubt,

Thomas Jefferson had kept a personal copy of the Koran in his library. Have you ever wondered why? It was to understand his enemies."

Daniel followed the procession as they pulled into the cemetery, where the cars continued to roll forward until they came to the gravesite. He put the car in park and turned to Saba. "But don't you think all of it is terrible? I mean this soldier had his whole life ahead of him but now he'll never get the chance to live it."

Saba placed his hand upon Daniel's shoulder. "Understand this one thing, my son: the soldier who falls on the field of battle never squanders his life. That blood spilt is holy because it is given in love, charity and duty for people that he will never meet who will enjoy the fruits of his sacrifice for generations to come. Whether you agree with his choice to serve his country is irrelevant. It was his choice and many others before who made the same choice that allow us to live in this nation, living free, and free to pursue the deepest desires of our hearts. That is the holiness of sacrifice. And make no mistake my son, it is necessary." Saba flashed a small smile before opening his door and stepping out.

Daniel followed the old man over to the gravesite, where the gathering of people was already thick. Saba took Daniel's hand and led him like a father through the crowd to stand in front of the casket draped with the national flag. The reds, whites, and blues shone brighter than Daniel had ever seen a flag do in the sunlight. His eyes stared. All his mind could do was think of one word: *holy*. He had never considered it before, but looking at the flag made him realize that the body of the young man beneath had shared more courage in his brief life than Dan had ever known. He could feel the blood rising from his chest, through his neck, and into his face making him hot and uncomfortable. It only took the briefest moments for him to realize the sensation of what he was feeling: shame.

The priest from the church again presided over the casket, canting in Arabic but with a contingent of Marines in their dress blues standing behind him at attention with their rifles. Daniel's eyes wandered down to the flag again, wondering what the soldier inside looked like and who he belonged to. He was beginning to feel genuinely sorry for the family's loss.

The strike of gunshots cracking the air shocked Dan from his reverie as he realized that a twenty-one gun salute was customary for an occasion like this one. Soldiers came up to the coffin and lifted the flag, folding it in their starched and methodical way into a triangle. The coffin was lowered into the ground and he could hear the sighing cries of women behind him and Saba, who stood steadfast.

One of the Marines then took the flag and stepped forward, standing directly in front of Saba. As he handed the coffin's flag to the old man, the soldier shared words of gratitude and deepest sympathy. Saba reached out and took the flag, acknowledging the words with a brief nod.

Daniel felt the blood in his face boil. He suddenly had the deepest regret for shooting his mouth off. It now occurred to him why the old man had been so detached all morning long. This fallen soldier was Saba's son Joshua.

Saba turned to face the crowd and as they gathered around him, he held up his hand and spoke aloud in Arabic. Every eyeball turned to look at Daniel, and he suddenly became very nervous, his knees began to shake. Then every person came and embraced Saba, giving him the customary kisses on each cheek, but to Daniel's surprise they came to him too, speaking in soft tones with words he couldn't begin to understand, and embracing him with kisses as well.

After the crowd departed, Daniel walked alongside Saba to the car. They each entered the vehicle and strapped in. Dan put the keys in the ignition and stopped. He turned his gaze upon the old man but he was having trouble seeing from the moisture in his eyes. "Saba...I'm so sorry."

Saba shook his head and shared a reassuring smile. "There's no need for apologies today."

Daniel wiped the tears from his eyes. "What did you say to them?"

"I told them you are now my son."

CHAPTER FOURTEEN

Dan found himself alone in the shop on a regular basis and several days had gone by without either Dan or Saba talking much. He didn't mind. Whenever the odd customer walked through the doors, he would put down his tools and assist them while covered in fine dust. At the moment, he brushed stain on the newly built book cases.

Bing. He heard the door open and so he put down the brush and stood up.

"It's just me Daniel. Shouldn't we be closed?" Saba said.

Dan glanced at his watch and realized that it was a half hour past due. He nodded and went over to the front of the store, turned the sign around so it said *closed* and then locked the front door. He closed up the can of stain and began rinsing out the paintbrush.

Saba popped up in front of him with a grin on his face. "Follow me. There's something I want to do."

Dan smiled while getting behind the old man. He realized that he had been asking fewer questions of late and had simply been happy to be where he was at. Things with Bridgette hadn't been very clear since their last meeting, but he was trying to find a way to resolve that.

Saba led them up the stairs, past the apartment flat, and up through the roof door where a table and two chairs had already been set out. The late summer sun set the sparse clouds ablaze with red and orange while starting to dip below the horizon. Saba indicated for Dan to sit and then joined him opposite at the table. The view of Pioneer Square was spectacular. Daniel saw Dodger shuffling past the store and around the corner out of eyeshot. He wondered where the ragamuffin man was going.

Dan was surprised to find a Cohiba cigar in his hand, placed there by Saba who was in the process of clipping his own before offering over the cigar trimmer. Daniel accepted it and smiled. The old man now pulled something out of his pocket resembling a mini blowtorch and *click*, lit up the cigar; then Daniel followed suit. Saba reached into a pack he carried up and took out two tumblers and a bottle of Elijah Craig bourbon. He poured three fingers full in each glass and handed one to Daniel.

"I didn't bring up any ice, but there's some in the kitchen if you would like."

Dan shook his head. "That's fine. I can take it neat." He sat back and puffed on the cigar. "So what is this all about?"

Saba took a sip of the bourbon and smiled. "It's about life, or rather the very little that I have left upon this earth."

"What?"

Saba nodded. "I'm sick and old. I'm sure you've noticed the odd appointments that I've been having, being out of the store so much. I've been visiting my doctor."

Dan's eyes were wide. "What is it?"

Saba's eyes softened to see his concern and he let out a sigh. "It's cancer, very advanced."

"Oh my God. When do you start the chemo?"

Saba shook his head. "I'm not going to do any treatments Daniel. There would be no reason for it. I'm old and I've lived a busy life. I have no fear of death and, to be perfectly honest, I am ready to be reunited with my family."

"But aren't I your family too? What about Deborah or Billy Pints?"

"Yes, you are all my children too. I have strived to get past my own convictions to learn to love people where they are at. It doesn't matter whether they are strippers, alcoholics, or homeless. They may be angry or depressed. But there's a secret I've found. We all have the same design. Every one of us has a soul with an all consuming hole in the center. This hole will eat up relationships, marriages, jobs, ambitions, and even our very lives unless it becomes filled with a presence greater than ourselves. God. He is the only one who can fill the spiritual vacuum inside us all."

Dan sat still, stunned.

"Are you all right Daniel?"

He shook his head. "No, I'm not all right."

"You'll be fine."

"I won't be fine. For the first time in my life I am in a place where I am happy both with myself and the world around me, only to find out *this*. Why won't you fight old man?"

Saba sighed and sipped his bourbon. "I will not fight this, Daniel, because death is not the end. It is rather a bridge to a new beginning. And I am ready to begin again."

"I don't want you to leave me," Dan said.

The old man shook his head and stared at him with his piercing black eyes. "I will never leave you. Don't you ever think that I would leave you because it will never happen."

"But when you die..."

"When I leave this earth, I shall have hoped to leave those around me in a better state than when I found them."

Dan's eyes were full of tears and Saba could see his confusion.

"My son, when we die there are no material possessions in this world that we can take with us, and yet there is something that we can take along: our relationships. The friendships we forge are spiritual bonds that do not break at death. Instead they have the power to leave a lasting impact after we depart. And I like to think that when I leave this earth, I will get to take some of that with me too...until I am able to reunite with those friends again."

Dan remained silent, puffing his cigar.

Saba smiled and took a sip of his bourbon. "You too are beginning to make some of these bonds with those around you. I've seen how you look at Dodger wandering around the square. I know how you've been reaching out to your wife despite the pain in your marriage. At some level inside, you get it my son. You will never be alone so long as you strive to love those around you. This is a lesson that I have paid dearly to learn."

Dan blew out smoke and then sipped his bourbon. His eyes glazed over and settled into an unfocused haze. What was he to do? He felt like he was just beginning to sort everything out; figuring out what was important from the rest of the crap that life threw at him.

The old man watched Daniel and started chuckling.

"What?" Dan said in monotone.

"Why do you look so long? You look like someone just told you that they have cancer." Saba laughed out loud and poured out more bourbon for Daniel and himself.

Daniel cracked the smile he was refusing to share and then joined in with a good laugh.

Saba puffed his cigar. "A joyful heart is good medicine, but a broken spirit dries up the bones. ~Proverbs 17:22."

Dan nodded. "I just have one question: what do I need to do?"

"How do you mean?"

"To help you. What do I need to do to help you?"

Saba sat back, rubbing his bald head with his spare hand.

"Is there anything I can do to help you ease your pain...if you are in pain?"

The old man nodded. "Yes. You can love those around you fiercely and undyingly. And you can start by returning love to those who seek to be close to you...regardless of how flawed they may be." Saba reached into a pocket and handed over an envelope.

Dan recognized the handwriting in his name on the front.

"Bridgette dropped this by a few days ago and asked me to give it to you when I thought you were ready. The truth is that we are never really ready to love those around us through the pain that they may cause, but the only way to become whole in the relationship is to do just that. We are commanded to defy our very natures if we want to nurse those broken souls into health. It is the essence of every spiritual struggle." Saba held up his glass in a toast. "We must die to ourselves everyday."

CHAPTER FIFTEEN

DANIEL STOOD STILL, watching the door. His eyes traveled over the entire frame of his house, or at least what was previously his home. Tap. Tap tap. He felt the start of the rain atop his head, which made up his mind for him. It seemed as though fate had conspired with the weather to urge him forward.

He crossed the street and made his way to the front door when he stopped and listened. There were voices arguing from inside. He stood as stone three moments longer before stepping back, changing his mind and turning to walk away but the front door burst open and an angry middle-aged blonde man stormed out. Daniel remained motionless, watching everything unfold, not wanting to interfere with the natural progression of events. The blonde man looked forward and his eyes connected with Dan's, and then they turned from anger to fear.

"I told you never to come back here!" Bridgette had run to the front door. She too saw Dan and began to cry.

"Good riddance to garbage!" yelled the man. "I am *never* coming back to your damn house again." He walked past Daniel. "She's a mess. You can have her."

"She was never yours to begin with," Dan spoke in the firmest voice, but it rang in his ears as something other than angry.

As the blonde man stormed away, Dan walked forward toward Bridgette crying at the front door.

"What are you doing here?" She said.

Daniel reached into his leather jacket and pulled out the envelope Saba had given him. "I've read it more than a dozen times."

Her wet eyes averted his gaze. "It probably sounds phony now, after what you just saw."

He held up the envelope. "No, I think it sounds honest. Even more honest after what I saw. Do you really mean what you wrote to me?"

The blonde curls on her head bobbed as she nodded. "Very much so. He just won't leave me alone."

"Let's not talk about him right now. Let's just talk about us." Dan reached out, placing a hand on her shoulder. "May I come in?"

"Yes. The house is a mess but otherwise..."

He smiled. "Thank you."

"Dinner's ready."

"I'll be there in just a moment," Dan called from upstairs. Stepping out of a steamy bathroom with a towel around his waste, he glance about for his clothes. He had not expected things to go this way, but something deep inside his chest purred with pleasure. His eyes traveled the room but his clothes were nowhere to be found, and certainly not on the floor where he had left them.

Bridgette now stood in the doorway, watching him.

"Where's my clothes?"

"In the wash. They were wet...and smelly. You've become so much of a man lately that you've even begun to stink like one."

"Yeah? How do you like them apples?"

"I'll get back to you on it."

"Well, if part of being a real man is being stinky, then I'll take it."

Dan laughed and she joined in. Her crystalline blue eyes sparkled, warming Dan in his core.

Bridgette walked over to the closet. "All the clothes you left behind are still here. Just wear something else."

Dan worked through the closet, choosing a gray T-shirt and jeans. "Look, I'm not sure what happened just now...well I don't know what it really means yet."

"I'm still trying to figure it out too. But I'd like to think that our intimacy can be the beginning of healing."

"Somehow we just needed each other. Yeah I feel that too," he said pulling his shirt over his head.

"So where are we now?" she asked.

Dan pointed to the envelope with her letter in it on the nightstand next to his jacket. "You've already apologized. All I really came here to do was to tell you that...I forgive you. I've been learning what it means to love others, and I mean *really love them*. None of this mamby-pamby-Hollywood-reach-out-and-love-the-world kind of crapola. I mean real love. Reaching out to the person next to me and letting them know that they are valuable, even if they're wearing rags. Having lunch with someone everybody else would consider a throw-away-person. And in return learning to accept love from others when it is offered freely with nothing attached—no agenda involved. And more importantly, learning to do all of this by overcoming my own judgments of other's faults and failures...including my own."

Bridgette's eyes were intense and focused. "Saba has done a lot for you hasn't he?"

"He's done everything for me. I don't know where I would be if he hadn't taken me in and given me a job and a place to heal. I've never met another man like him."

She nodded. "He's shown you how to live?"

"More," Dan said and came over to give her a hug. "He's shown me what is worth living for. That all the stuff we spend our lives chasing after leads nowhere, but investing in relationships can have eternal consequences so we need to make the most of loving those in our lives."

She drew herself deep into his embrace. "You have changed. I wish I could be like that."

"That's the purpose, sweetie. If love doesn't change us for the better—then it's not love." He kissed her forehead. "And if we aren't sacrificing something of ourselves to do it, then we are trapped in prisons of our own making."

She giggled. "You sound funny talking all smart and philosophical."

"The old man is rubbing off on me. I can only hear him chatter on with his nutty ideas for so long before they start setting in."

"Well I'm glad for that above all else."

"Me too. So what's for dinner?"

CHAPTER SIXTEEN

THE OLD POWDER blue GTO drove like a champ on the freeway, and Dan liked being behind the wheel. A casual glance over towards Saba in the passenger seat caused him to smile at the way the old man watched everything passing by, as if he were trying to make the most of every moment.

"So I couldn't help but notice that you have been spending quite a few nights away from the store," Saba said without looking in Daniel's direction. "How's your wife?"

"You couldn't help yourself," Dan said with a laugh.

Saba turned his penetrating gaze upon him, a thin but serious smile playing upon his lips. "Of course not. You're my son."

Those words warmed Dan from the core. He didn't realize how much it meant to hear it. He cleared his throat. "She's, uh, good."

"And how are you with this new situation?"

Dan nodded. "Good too. I mean this feels good, or right...or whatever."

Saba turned his gaze back outside. "Is she healing?"

"I don't know what you mean."

"Her heart has incurred much damage, both from her own choices and the choices of others. Is she working to heal her wounds?"

Dan didn't look at Saba, but kept his hands on the steering wheel, his knuckles turning white. "I don't know what you mean."

"It's a simple question. You should be able to tell."

"Well, I can't tell because I'm not a mind reader. What are you getting at Saba?"

The old man sat still, breathing from one moment to the next, then spoke in a kind but firm voice. "What I am getting at is this: you can't do this on your own."

"What?"

"Neither can she. And you can't do it together either, otherwise things will come apart again."

Dan's eyes turned cold as he looked over to Saba. "Explain yourself."

"If you try to fix her, she will break. If she tries to fix you, you will break. Broken people cannot mend each other alone. There must be more."

"More what?"

Saba pointed a knobby finger ahead, where his church came into view. "Park first."

Dan drove onto the parking lot and settled the GTO in a spot. Saba opened his door and stood up, motioning for Dan to join him. The two men walked into the church, but Dan's head was swimming. He couldn't tell if Saba was judging him or not...but there were questions that needed answering. They sat side by side in an old pew, but the old man said nothing. The service began in it's ritualistic Melkite style with the standing and the sitting, and the proclamations and responses in Arabic. Dan followed through with Saba, but still didn't have a clue what it was all about. He kept silent and soaked it all in, not letting his lips open once so as not to disturb the melodic flow.

The mass finished and Daniel and Saba climbed back into the car. Once on the road, Saba pointed to a Dick's Drive-in and they picked up a couple of cheeseburgers with fries. Daniel couldn't hold the suspense any longer.

"What do you mean there needs to be more?" He asked.

The old man chewed thoughtfully and swallowed. "Still stuck on that are we?"

"Well, you didn't exactly make it clear the first time."

Saba nodded. "I suppose so. My apologies." He sipped his soda and cleared his throat. "Have you ever considered why marriage ceremonies traditionally are held in a holy place such as a church, synagogue, mosque, etc...?"

Dan shrugged his shoulders. "I hadn't really thought about it before. I always considered that it was just the prettiest place to hold a wedding. But perhaps it has something to do with faith?"

"Exactly," Saba said and turned his black eyes on Daniel. "Marriage is about more than a lifetime commitment between two people. It is sacred. Holy ground that not only binds two earthly souls together but also binds them to God. That is why the weddings are traditionally held in holy places. Marriages are not just about the bonding of two souls, because there is a third party involved: God."

Dan laughed, "so what you're saying is that marriage involves three people?"

"In a matter of spiritually speaking, yes. God is meant to be involved and to intervene among two committed but broken souls, to make them new. I am certain that the institution of marriage was specifically designed to bring a glimpse of heaven into earthly existence, no matter the religion, culture, or creed."

Dan sat for several moments in his own thoughts, trying to digest Saba's words. "And what about other religions—other faiths? Do those paths also lead to God?"

Saba shook his head. "I have read much of the world's literature and have come to very few solid conclusions. Most of the world's paths have been conspicuously devised by men over the millenia. The twelve steps of Buddhism. The five pillars of Islam. The five thousand additional laws of the Talmud surrounding the original 613 laws in the Torah. Even the concepts of penance within Catholic tradition all originally stemmed from men adding their vision onto what they thought was God's plan for humanity. And much of it shares notions about earning forgiveness. Yet the one unshakeable thing I know is this: forgiveness cannot be earned, only given. We may become lost in traveling down any which path to find God, but it is always he who ultimately finds us, broken, wherever we are. And all we have to do to begin anew is to accept his forgiveness, which he gives us freely."

"What is it he wants in return? I've never understood how God could give us anything for free. What is it he wants?" Dan said.

Saba smiled. "Relationship. He desires to know us, and for us to know him. And we are created in his image. That is why he created man as social beings. That is why man creates a family, joins society, and even builds cities. And it is also why God made marriage, to foster the development of the future of his creation. And he is directly involved every step of the way."

"So when you say that Bridgette and I need more, then what we need is...to include God in our marriage?"

Saba nodded and then took another big bite of his cheeseburger.

CHAPTER SEVENTEEN

THE DAY WAS used cleaning up and running *Olde Mysterium*. Dan wanted to spend a couple of days in rest regarding the shop's repairs. The newly stacked bookcases stood in a formation Dan thought made the store feel more inviting, showing more books toward the front windows. He swept, and wiped down walls, dusted shelves and furniture, and assisted the occasional customer. He even began reading the book of John on his spare time, but kept that secret to himself lest the old man find out about it, who was away from the store again. Dan stopped asking questions but knew Saba was at the doctor's office.

A grin crept wide across his face as he thought about Bridgette. Dan felt as if their relationship had begun afresh; new love all over. He spent every night of the week at home...their home. In the deepest chambers of his heart he knew he wanted things to work out, and so he kept working on himself and opening up to her. Dan was surprised to find her doing the same. Yet somehow Saba's words kept rolling around in his head like a handful of loose marbles. *We need to include God.* The thought made him uncomfortable and Bridgette had never been much of the churchgoing type, although he knew that her family had when she was a little girl.

Dan felt the strange sensation that he had become comfortable with God–or at least with the idea or concept of God hanging around. After all, the old man had a tendency to chatter on about life philosophy, love, psychology, but mostly he just talked about Jesus. It was fascinating to Dan how something like Jesus would have turned him completely off in his former, very comfortable life. Yet now he couldn't seem to shake it. Or him. Or whatever. Perhaps crisis can be a catalyst for faith, or at least it was for Dan.

He shook off his thoughts, realizing that he was going a bit too deep. How did that happen? The old man wasn't even around. Dan sighed a small laugh, happy to be thinking happy thoughts again...even if it was just about Jesus.

The bell chimed it's hovered pitch through the store from it's perch above the front door. Dan stashed his duster underneath the register counter. "Can I help you?" he called out.

"Only if you have a parcel for pickup," came the reply from a lovely voice; a voice with strength in its own singsong way. Deborah emerged from the book racks to the counter, a wide grin upon her face.

"I don't believe we've ever met."

"Nope. Not officially." She shook her head and stuck out her hand, saying her name.

Dan replied with his own name and shook her hand. "Now I'm not sure about a parcel," he said as he looked underneath the counter. "Saba didn't tell me about one anyway."

She pointed with a long finger. "They're usually in the office. Check the bookshelf next to the desk, I've seen him get them from there sometimes."

Dan looked and found a parcel wrapped in brown paper and tied with string. The old man did certain things in such an old fashioned way, that he found himself smiling without realizing. When he brought it out, he was struck by Deborah's sharp features, any one of which alone would seem quirky but when combined shared an austere loveliness. "Where do you take these anyway?"

She held the package in her hands, looking down upon it. "Why don't you come along and find out?"

"I don't know...I mean the store..."

"Will be fine without you," she said in a matter of fact tone.

He thought about it two moments longer and then decided to follow her. The feeling deep in his gut told him that he wanted to talk to her about Saba. Dan took his keys and locked the front door, following Deborah into the square across the street.

"So where do you take these packages anyway?" He asked.

She smiled and raised her thin, dark eyebrows. "I actually just take them to the post office for shipping."

Dan chuckled. "Then why am I following you? Why didn't you just tell me that?"

"Because I know something is on your mind."

So many things swirled around in Dan's head, the foremost being that he knew she had worked at Déjà Vu before Saba rescued her. "What was it like for you?"

Her smile sweetened, as if reading his thoughts, and she exhaled. "It was hard to work as a dancer. Demoralizing in fact. Most mornings I just went home and couldn't wait to shower and then sleep all day so I didn't have to think about it. Then I would wake up and do it all again."

"Why did you do it?"

Now she frowned. "Mostly because I needed to. I ran away from home when I was just seventeen. My family atmosphere was not overtly abusive, but extremely controlling. I made some wrong choices and some wrong turns along the way. Dancing was what I could do to make ends meet until I could figure things out. But the money becomes so easy that most women just stay because it works. At least that's what I did."

They walked along in silence for a bit before Dan added in. "Where are you sending the books that Saba gives you?"

"They go all over the world to buyers who have bought them. This particular parcel is going to Sotheby's for auction. It's a very rare set of three volumes printed in the late Renaissance about the banking history of the Italian city states."

"Why do you help him? I mean why can't Saba do this?"

She shrugged. "I don't have to help him. I want to. I do it because I love Saba in the way I wish I could have loved my father. I help him figure out which books are valuable and then I help him find the best place to sell them. It's sort of a hobby we both share together. Anyway it gives him a bit a pocket change, and he helps me pay for my tuition at Seattle Pacific University."

Dan whistled. "Sotheby's means more than just pocket change."

She glanced his way. "You have no idea."

Dan realized that there were so many things about Saba he knew nothing about. The old man was a veritable treasure trove of secret interests. "How do you handle the way he rambles on about faith? I mean *his* faith?"

Deborah let out a little laugh. "Very well. In fact Saba's faith is what saved me from my personal hell. I attribute everything he does because of his faith. A faith in God. And a faith in God's ability to work miracles in the everyday lives of broken hearts. That's what happened to me. Saba met me in Déjà Vu and it took a year for him to talk me into leaving. At that time I was involved in a very unhealthy relationship with a married man and it was Saba who convinced me that I am worth so much more. I learned that I was more valuable than what I was doing and he offered to show me a better way. His faith was not only a part of that, but as I found out, it was everything."

Dan nodded. "I know what you mean."

"Do you?" She stopped and looked directly at him. "Because it took a while for me to figure out what it really meant. There was one night when I was so broken that I felt tore up inside. Like my soul was ripped to shreds. At that time I was living in the apartment above the bookstore, just like you are now. The store was closed and I was all alone. Something took hold of me and I just broke down, crying harder than I had ever known I could—barely able to catch my breath. And feeling worthless. Somehow, it was almost divine, Saba showed up at the store to check up on me and he just held me. Cradling my head as if I were his own child. Whispering words of comfort and strength into the void that was my heart. It was then I learned what I needed to know most. The secret to my healing."

Dan's eyes were wide. "What?"

Deborah's gaze shifted into the distance, as if seeing something far off. "That Saba's faith is more than just belief. He embodies it. There was a part of him I could finally see that is completely occupied by Jesus Christ. His savior is the driving force in everything he does, and Saba can do some amazing things which has nothing to do with who he is, but rather because of who lives within his heart."

Dan agreed. He knew Saba could do some amazing things. The old man's love for those around him was supernatural.

"And yet there's more. I finally figured out that in order for me to heal and grow, I needed to have Saba's savior live within me too. I needed Jesus Christ in my life so badly, and yet it never occurred to me before that moment. So that is exactly what I did. I prayed. I asked for forgiveness. And I asked for Jesus to live within me—to make me whole. And he has done more than I could ever ask because I found that allowing God to forgive me allowed me to forgive myself. And ultimately it allows me to completely forgive others for the pain they have caused in my life. It is the cycle of forgiveness. A cycle of love. And a path for hope."

Daniel's mind reeled at the revelation. It was the missing link; the final piece of a puzzle that allowed him to see the whole picture and he wondered at why he couldn't see it before because it was so obvious. Jesus lived within the old man. It was no wonder why Saba couldn't stop talking about God, faith, and Jesus—because those things were alive within him. He now understood what the old man meant by the fact that he needed to include God into his marriage. He needed Saba's savior to live within him.

CHAPTER EIGHTEEN

DAN GLANCED UP at the old clock and saw the large hand approaching the top, almost time to close.

The front door chimed and his eyes skimmed over but he couldn't see who had entered the store. "Just fair warning," he called out. "We're about to close in five minutes."

"That's all right. I can wait." The sweet and familiar voice sounded as Bridgette emerged from the book racks, walking up to the counter.

Dan leaned over and gave her a kiss. The conversation he'd had earlier that day with Deborah remained in his thoughts, unshakeable, immovable. "I was just thinking about seeing you tonight. There's some things I need to talk to you about."

Her fair cheeks blushed. "Then let's go get some coffee."

Daniel turned off the lights and locked the front door, then he offered an arm to his wife and they strolled down the sidewalk together. The night air was pleasant but the gathered clouds overhead promised rain at some point. They strolled through the square and around the corner up to the neighborhood cafe, where Dan ushered her inside and they took a table next to the window.

"Your usual?" She asked and then went up to the counter after Dan nodded.

He thought, turning himself inside out on how to talk to her about this stuff. How could he tell her that he had come to a crossroads, unable to be milquetoast any longer about what it means to have faith? About what it means to live a life of faith? He hadn't made any official declaration or anything. Dan simply knew that he had come to a decision; one which would ultimately affect their marriage—either for the better or the worse depending on how she handled the news. Bridgette came back with their lattes and placed one before him.

He turned his cup round and again in his hands before even taking his first sip. Why was he so nervous? This was silly. "Hey Bridgette, I just feel that there is something we need to talk about...I mean I need to share with you." His gaze traveled from the tabletop to her face, which was unusually pale. "Are you all right?"

Bridgette placed a hand to her mouth and ran to the bathroom. Dan's stomach churned as his concern for her rose. He sensed she had been noticeably quiet, more than usual that evening. He sipped his latte and waited.

She returned to her seat with her usual grace of motion, but he could tell that she was not feeling well.

"Look, we should get you home and into bed. I can make us both some soup. How long have you been like this?" he said.

She nodded and sipped her coffee. "A little while I guess."

"Okay, well let's go home. I'll tuck you in and–"

Her hand reached across the table and rested upon his arm. "No, I wanted us to come here tonight." She took a deep breath. "I know that you have something you need to discuss, but there's something that's come up and I need to let you know about it."

Dan's heart sank into his stomach. "What's going on? Is it–you know...him?"

She shook her head. "No, no. Nothing like that." But then her head tilted sideways.

Dan attempted to read her body language, read her mood, read anything that might give it away. But he couldn't do it. He had never been really good at reading women, especially the one sitting in front of him. He kept silent, sipped his coffee and looked into her eyes. Full attention.

She looked sideways and behind, softly spinning her cup but never drinking its contents. "I don't know how it happened. I mean, I know how it happened–it's just that..." Her eyes found his and she straightened up, as if screwing up her courage. "I'm pregnant."

Dan's face brightened, a smile wide and brimming. This was their chance. It was as if destiny had helped to seal the deal and make sure their marriage continued. But as these thoughts crossed his mind he could see her expression remaining somber, and then his stomach dropped like a stone. He could sense there was more.

"Bridgette, this should be good news. So what's wrong?"

She shook her head. "I'm nearing the end of my first trimester."

Dan stared openly back at her, not understanding.

"Dan, I'm at the end of my third month. I'm so sorry. I never meant to keep this from you, but we just started getting together and making things happen...you and I..."

And then he understood. As she kept talking, he tuned her out because it was clear that this pregnancy was not wanted in more than one way. "Who's the father?" His question seemed blank and hollow.

Bridgette shook her head and her blonde curls bobbed, but couldn't hide the tears now streaming down her face. "I'm so sorry. I'm such a horrible person and if you want to end this all right now—I wouldn't blame you."

"Who's the father?"

She turned her eyes down. "I don't know."

Dan now leaned forward. His ears were on fire and the pulse in his neck throbbed. "Bridgette, who's the father?"

She now burst into complete sobbing. Through her mumbled cries came, "there's a small chance it could be you, but in all reality..."

"It's probably *him*." Dan spoke in a quiet, matter-of-fact tone. "Shit, I knew this was too good to be true. Just too many things in a row turning out right." He looked at her face, but could not meet her gaze as her eyes remained averted. "When were you going to tell me?"

"I wasn't. I went and found a doctor who could, you know, take care of it."

"You mean an abortion?"

Her face scrunched at the word and her shoulders hunched. "Yes, I mean that very thing."

"Then why didn't you?"

She licked her lips. "Because there's a chance it could be yours. I couldn't bring myself to end a life that is made with the man that I love."

"Oh so you're talking about me now?" Dan spat and then retreated. He rubbed his temples. "I'm sorry, that was uncalled for."

"No, no. I deserve it. I deserve it all. And you deserve so much better than me."

Dan sat for a moment, trying to collect his thoughts. His coffee was going cold but he no longer had any desire to drink it. "So what do we do now?"

"I'm still going to have the doctor remove it. And I can see that it would be best if we both moved forward—separately. We could never heal our marriage Daniel, it just wasn't ever possible. You were right to leave in the first place, but I do want to tell you that I am thankful."

"For what?" He asked, completely disarmed with the turn their conversation was taking.

"For giving me a second chance. But I didn't deserve it." She leaned over and gave him a kiss on the forehead. "I release you Daniel. You don't have to keep trying anymore. Not at all for my sake. But I do want you to be happy, and so I need to let you go."

CHAPTER NINETEEN

Days passed along in a fuzzy emotional stupor and Dan realized one morning that he didn't know what to do, and he had no idea what he was doing. The conversation he had shared with Deborah was still present, but it's prominence in his mind waned in the background. He wanted to feel angry, and although he tried he found that it wasn't there. Instead he felt sorry both for Bridgette and himself. His head told him that her leaving was the right thing to do, but his heart ached all the same and without any particular reason or understanding.

Saba had been in and out of the store as was his usual routine, but he seemed to notice Dan's dissonance and said nothing more to him in passing but simple conversation. Dan also noticed the old man gave him more space than was usually the case. His eyes glanced around the store and he admired his handiwork. The lights were warm and even; the craggy brick wall imparted an ageless feel, and the newly stained book cases and floor reflected darkly the warm humor of the lights. Then he found himself looking at Saba, who was doing the same thing.

"This is some very fine work my son. You should be proud of yourself."

Dan nodded. He was proud of himself and it helped to lift his spirit, if only a little.

Saba cocked an eye at him, as if his wheels were turning. "Let me ask you something. Do you think this store needs something else? Something to bring in more people? To make it inviting?"

Dan had been thinking about this for the past month but hadn't brought it up to Saba because he didn't want to stretch whatever the old man's budget was. "Um actually, I was thinking that it would be really great to build an espresso over there." Dan pointed to the front of the store, where there was a reading spot by the windows. "That space could be put to better use. And if people passing by see an espresso bar happening, they would be more likely to come in. It's all about atmosphere. A third place, if you will."

"Third place?" Saba asked, his white eyebrows arched.

"A third place. Home is the first place. Work is the second place. People need a third place to go when they want to escape for a short while; a place to meet with friends and relax."

Saba nodded, placing his finger upon the center of his chin, his black eyes fixed to the very spot that Dan suggested. "I like it. You are right Daniel, the books in this place are too old and musty to make the store feel friendly. You're espresso bar could bring fresh life to *Olde Mysterium*. Please start on it right away."

A smile crept over Dan's face as he looked from the old man to the spot of the new project by the front windows. Saba turned away and went into the back office. Dan felt the internal tug in his direction. He walked forward, trying to think of what to say, or how to say it. Dan needed guidance. He knew that he needed his... "Father?" The word slipped from his lips before he even knew what he was saying.

Saba looked up from his seat at the desk, his face seemed more tired than normal but his smile was wide, genuine, and full of love. "Yes, my son?"

Dan's soul spilled forth. "I need your help. I'm so confused and I don't know what to do."

"This sounds serious," Saba said sitting back in his chair. "What seems to be the problem?"

Dan shook his head, not sure how to formulate the words, but he figured that he would just let it out. No control. "Bridgette's pregnant."

Saba exhaled relief. "You had me worried there for a moment. I thought you were going to tell me that you were stricken with a life-threatening disease. Maybe cancer."

"That's not funny."

Saba chuckled. "Please forgive my dark sense of humor. But I can see that you are troubled somehow. So I must ask you, why is the child she carries a burden? I thought that you and your wife were mending your commitment. A child is the ultimate product of a loving marriage."

"That's not the point," Dan shook his head. "The child may not be mine."

"I see. So where do you go from here?"

Dan ran his fingers through his hair. "That's just it. I feel so torn. Bridgette let me go. She said that I was right in the first place to leave and that she wasn't worthy of our love."

Saba scratched the thick white stubble on his jaw and closed his eyes, thinking. "Nobody's worthy of love, my son. None of us are worthy of it, which is why love is so beautiful. We desire it, we are built for it, and we feel the need to give it, but ultimately not one person on earth is worthy of receiving love. But we receive it anyway because it is gifted to us."

"I understand that, but still the child may not be mine."

Saba thought for a moment. "I understand your concern but I would ask you to consider this: you love your wife."

"Of course I do, but what has that got to do with...?"

"I'm not finished," Saba said and exhaled. "You love Bridgette and the baby that she carries might not be of your blood but is certainly of hers. And her child is innocent regarding the circumstances of its conception, but will need a loving family regardless. If you truly love your wife, then her child is yours as well."

Dan remained motionless and uncertain.

Saba's brow furrowed as he looked up at Dan. "You are not of my blood, yet you are my son. I have loved you and sheltered you as my own, and therefore you belong to me."

"But that's different," Dan said.

"How?"

"Because I was not born of your wife."

Saba chuckled. "That's true. Okay so how about this: have you ever considered the circumstances surrounding Jesus Christ's birth? I know you've been reading the gospels."

Dan shook his head, there was nothing he could keep secret from the old man. "Go on."

"The truth is that Jewish culture two thousand years ago was very different from our modern age. When the New Testament speaks of Joseph being engaged to Mary, what we don't understand from our own perspective is that engagements lasted one year, where the couple lived as husband and wife but their marriage was not consummated until a year later upon their wedding. So somewhere within that year, Mary became pregnant through the Holy Spirit. You following so far?"

Dan nodded.

"Good. So do you know what Joseph could have done? He had the full right to drag her into the street and bring her before the courts. He could have demanded her to be stoned to death, and the courts very well might have complied. Yet he did nothing of the sort, in fact the gospels refer to Joseph as a righteous man who was going to divorce her quietly and send her away. It wasn't until he was confronted by an angel of the Lord explaining the circumstances of her pregnancy that Joseph reconsidered the engagement and decided to follow through with the wedding anyway. Why? The child Mary carried was not of his blood yet Joseph agreed to marry her anyway and raise her son as his own."

Dan shook his head, "I don't know if I can do that."

Saba placed a hand on Daniel's shoulder, "of course you can. Joseph did it because he was filled with compassion and love for Mary. You can do it because you too are filled with compassion and love for Bridgette."

Dan's eyes felt hot as tears leaked into them, obscuring his vision. "But I can't do it alone. I can't do this on my own." He sank to his knees and hugged the old man around the midsection. "Saba you are so kind to all and a friend to everyone who is lucky enough to know you. I don't know why because you have suffered more pain and loss than anyone else I know. You should be angry at life and at the world yet you love with complete abandon. You love with a fierce courage that I don't understand, and yet I wish I could have it too."

Saba kissed Daniel on the top of the head and placed his hands there. "But you can have it Daniel. All you have to do is ask for it."

"How?" Daniel's eyes looked upward at the old man but couldn't see him through the boiling tears.

Saba knelt down and joined Daniel on the floor. "Then pray with me my son."

"What should I say?"

"Just follow after me: Jesus you are the master mender of broken people. Please mend me and make me whole so that I may love everyone around me in such a way that there will be no doubt you are the Lord of my life. Enter into my life now and leave me never and make me into the man you created me to become."

CHAPTER TWENTY

DAN CLOSED THE door to the GTO and walked up the steps to his house. The lights were on and so he knew she would be home. The snow drifted around him in minuscule glowing orbs but he paid them no mind. He held the key to his front door, but instead of unlocking the door, he placed it back in his pocket and knocked. His heart raced for what felt an eternity before he heard the door unlock from the other side and open.

Bridgette stood motionless, her expression agog.

"Can we talk?" Dan said.

She remained in the doorway for several heartbeats more but then stepped aside. Dan entered and they both went into the kitchen.

"What do you want to know?" She said as she leaned over the counter.

Dan sat in a bar stool on the other side. "Do you love me?"

Her face remained stoic for several moments, but then her forehead creased and gave way to emotion. "Of course I do, but I'm the one..."

Dan held up his hand to stop her and then he took a breath. "This world is full of people doing terrible things to each other, doing everything they can to show the opposite of love. But the amazing thing is that every one of them wants love in the worst way possible yet none are deserving." He took her hand in his. "Nobody is deserving of love. None of us. Not one. But I've learned that when love is given freely, with no strings attached, it can heal wounds. And we are only able to receive love when it is given freely."

Bridgette's eyes watered. "I don't understand what you're saying Daniel."

He leaned forward and kissed her hand. "What I'm saying is this: I choose to love you freely. No strings attached. We are both free of our past."

"But I'm not free of my past. I have an appointment at the end of this week to end my pregnancy. There's nothing about that which I can leave behind."

"You're right. We can't leave it behind, but we can move forward...what if you and I kept the baby?"

Tears now ran freely down her face. "What are you saying? This baby's not even yours. Most likely."

"Maybe not, but the baby is yours Bridgette. And I choose to love you with all abandon. So your baby is mine too. If your name is to be on the birth certificate, then I want mine there as well."

Bridgette pulled her hand away from his. "What has gotten into you?"

Dan said nothing but simply smiled at her with every measure of compassion and passion that overflowed from his soul.

Her blue eyes scanned him, tears still running down her flushed cheeks. "I can't see anything about you that I recognize Daniel. Even your gray eyes look brighter somehow."

"I'm not the same guy who walked out on you. That man was torn and busted up and overflowing with anger. After our conversation at the coffee shop, I tried to get angry. I tried. But there was nothing left because it had been exhausted and removed. Instead it was replaced by something that is totally new to me. And after Saba helped me talk it through, I finally understood what it was."

"What?"

His hands reached out again and took hers. "Genuine love. For the first time in my life I've found that I can care about people without expecting anything in return. I've found that I care about you the most, and you'll never be expected to give anything in return." He paused for breath. "Bridgette, there is nothing that you can do to ever make me stop loving you."

Fresh tears flowed freely and now she ran to the other side of the counter and hugged her husband. "But why? I still don't understand the 'why' of it all. Everything you're saying is wonderful, but I can never stand up to it all Daniel."

"You're not supposed to Lovely." He hadn't called her by that name in a long time and it felt good to say it. "It's just supposed to be a gift."

Bridgette sobbed but couldn't get any words through.

"Let me ask you something. You say you still love me?"

She nodded.

"Then how about we just take it a day at a time. One day. Each day. Everyday."

Bridgette settled down a bit. "Really?"

"For the rest of our lives. I don't ever want to spend another night away from you, my love. I will never leave your side again."

She nestled her head against his shoulder. "I wish I could have whatever it is that's gotten into you."

Daniel chuckled. "But you can. We aren't meant to do this alone Bridgette. I never understood what Saba meant by that until recently. It's a beautiful thing."

"Can you tell me about it?"

CHAPTER TWENTY ONE

THE MORNING CAME quickly and Dan parked the GTO behind *Olde Mysterium*. The remainder of last night's snow on the ground refused to melt due to the crisp clear sky. Streets that should have been busy were abandoned sheets of blanketed white fluff. Dan was always amazed at how a city so busy and used to wet weather could now just abruptly halt because of a few inches of snow.

He entered through the rear entrance and went straight up to the front door, which he unlocked before peering out the windows. There was no one about and he could tell it was going to be one of those days. Dan walked back into the kitchen and poured water into the coffee maker before setting himself to the task of grinding fresh beans into a black, robustly aromatic powder. He hadn't yet started the espresso bar, but Dan fought internally over whether that project should start today or not. He decided that he could figure it out after a hot cup and spending some time watching nothing outside through the front windows. While waiting for the coffee to finish brewing, he heard the front door chime and open.

Dan poked his head around the corner and saw Deborah coming toward him. "Hey, I don't think there are any packages. I looked this morning."

Her head shook and her eyes were bloodshot. "I couldn't figure out how to get a hold of you last night. You weren't here and I don't know where your house is."

"What is it? What's wrong?"

Tears formed in the corners of her eyes. "Saba was taken to the hospital last night. He's been asking for you."

Dan locked up the shop and left a sign regarding family emergency. He and Deborah climbed into the GTO and motored as fast as they could up Pill Hill to Swedish Hospital.

The hospital wasn't packed with patients, but the staff teemed the halls with a collective sense of urgency and duty as if bees in a hive. Deborah led them through the maze of hallways and up the elevator and through more hallways until she motioned to one door, and Dan walked through it.

The room was bare with sparse settings of uncomfortable looking furniture. Saba laid in the bed, arms folded over his chest which rose and fell in outstretched intervals. Dan sat in a metal chair and reached across to hold the old man's hand which was cool to the touch. Deborah stood in the doorway and both of them watched with reverence.

"What happened last night?" Dan spoke barely above a whisper.

Deborah shifted. "We were leaving church and going to get dinner when he said he was in pain and so I brought him here. He didn't look like he was in a lot of pain but they admitted him immediately when he described his symptoms."

Dan nodded his head and continued to watch.

"You don't have to talk about me like I'm not here." Saba's eyes opened and he looked over at Daniel. "My son, you have finally come."

"I'm so sorry. I would've come last night if I had known—"

Saba waved his free hand. "Your business last night was more important than attending to my old bones."

"But that's not true," Dan said, tears obscuring his vision.

"But it is. You talked to Bridgette last night? You shared everything?"

Dan nodded.

"You both will keep and raise the baby?"

"Yes."

"You have saved a life. Your business was more important."

Dan squeezed Saba's hand. "That's only because you saved mine first."

"And you in turn have saved mine, Daniel. You entered my life at one of its darkest chapters during the loss of my...other son. Your inquisitive nature and sweat transformed *Olde Mysterium* from a musty bookstore into something more relevant, more beautiful; and that will forever be some of my best cherished memories. And you have also transformed yourself and changed hopelessness into hope. You stepped from a life like death into a life worth living, and I was honored to be there and see you do it. I didn't change you my son. You allowed yourself to be changed by someone greater than us all."

Dan bowed his head and let the tears fall on the bed. "Jesus."

"Yes, my son. Jesus has transformed you. He has a knack for taking something broken and making it new again."

Deborah announced that she would go find the doctor to ask for a status update.

Saba closed his eyes and breathed deep. "My time here on this earth is coming quickly to a close. Oh how fast it has fled me. Have you ever wondered at how people are engineered for eternity?"

"I don't understand."

"I have never met an old man that didn't wish he could live longer. Eighty years. Ninety years. Even a century old. It doesn't matter. We might want to go to end the pain but never because we are finished with life. The human spirit is engineered to want to live. To live forever. We don't understand it. I don't understand it because our experience on this earth is designed to be finite. Everything here has an expiration date except the human spirit."

Saba's face pulled taut into a mass of wrinkles for a moment but then subsided. Daniel offered to go find a nurse but the old man protested, keeping his grip firm on his son's hand.

"Will you do something for me?"

Daniel nodded. "Absolutely. Anything you want."

"Kneel by my bedside."

Daniel did as he was bade. Saba pushed himself up into a sitting position with a burden of effort and then placed both hands on Dan's head. The old man spoke gently at first in his native tongue. Dan couldn't understand the words but soaked in the love from them. Then Saba continued in English. "Oh Lord my God, King of the Universe, may you make my son to be like Jesus the Messiah and our Salvation. Give him your strength that he may be a warrior of love, fiercely defending those around him from the encroaching darkness of this present world. Oh great and wonderful Mystery of Old, may you keep my son and bless him. May your hand be upon him and give him the peace that surpasses all understanding."

Saba then lifted Dan's face and looked into his eyes. "This is my blessing for you and the greatest inheritance I can bestow upon you Daniel. I love you as I love myself. And the greatest desire of my heart at this very moment is to be able to see you again at the end of time and all things."

Dan opened his mouth but his throat closed up. He cleared it before being able to barely get something out. "It will be done."

Dan stood up and hugged his father, loving the man in his arms in a way that he had never before experienced. It was something bright, pure, and warm. And he wanted more.

A nurse walked into the room and right up to the bed. "All right Mr. Ghazal, you need to lay down now and get some rest." She looked at Dan. "Visiting hours are over, only family are allowed."

"I am family. I'm his son." Dan said and held back the fresh supply of tears threatening to erupt.

The nurse looked at both men and shrugged her shoulders. "Well then keep your father in bed. He shouldn't be exciting himself. Mr. Ghazal, do you need something more to relieve the pain?"

Saba shook his head.

"All right then, I'll be back in another hour." And with that she left.

Saba turned his black eyes back toward Daniel. "Go home and share your love with your wife."

Dan nodded, the tears now flowing again. "See you tomorrow?"

"Yes."

CHAPTER TWENTY TWO

DAN RETURNED TO the hospital the next morning after a fitful night of sleep. He took the elevator up and walked through the labyrinthine hallways until he reached the room he had visited the day before. Dan poked his head into the room but did not find what he had expected. His eyes beheld a room that was sterile, fresh, and empty.

He flagged down the nearest passing nurse. "Where is he?"

"He who sweetie?" Her grandmotherly aire showed in her speech.

Dan motioned to the empty room. "Saba Ghazal. The patient that was in this room last night.

The nurse's forehead pulled into a fret of wrinkles and but her eyes remained clear. "I'm so sorry, but Mr. Ghazal passed in the night. May I ask who you are?"

"I'm his son."

The nurse attempted to make more conversation, but Dan simply turned away and left. As he departed the hospital, his mind spun and his heart ached but he could not yet grieve. It would take some time for it all to sink in and process before he was ready for any output. He drove the GTO through downtown until he came upon Pioneer Square, where he pulled the car around behind the shop and parked.

He turned the key and let himself in through the back door. He turned on the lights and then it hit him. What was going to happen to this place? This store of knowledge that Saba had spent a lifetime collecting seemed to now hang in the balance. Dan's eyes wandered about at his handiwork but now he began to look at the books. Really look at them. As if seeing them for the first time. All of them old. All of them used. Some had begun to fall into disrepair and he could see the stealthy handiwork to keep them together; Dan could only assume that Saba had facilitated the restoration.

Knocking came from the front door and Dan walked his way over and unlocked it, letting Deborah through.

"Did you go see him yet this morning?" she asked.

He shook his head.

"Should we go see him together?"

Dan again shook his head. "He's not there."

Deborah gazed deep into Dan's expression and then showed that she too now understood. "So he is finally reunited with his beloved. Somehow I feel like the light in my life dimmed a bit."

"Yeah. I know without Saba, I might still be in my darkness. He brought his light into my life and it remains still even though he has left." Dan ran his fingers through his hair. "Would you like some coffee?"

"Can I show you something?" Deborah's eyes glistened and her mouth upturned in a slightly bitter smile, yet Dan could easily read the love upon her face. He nodded and followed her to a table where she laid down her satchel and pulled out a file. Her smile widened before handing it to him.

"What is this?"

Deborah said not a word. Her eyes simply glanced at the file and then back at Dan. With a sigh, he sat down and opened it. Inside were small stacks of legal typed documents that had been notarized and signed by

Saba as well as a sealed envelope with Dan's name printed on the front. Dan glanced through the documents and recognized that it was a will. Moreover he saw that his own name was listed as the *only* beneficiary.

Fresh tears welled up and he wiped them away. "What does this mean Deborah?"

"It means that Saba Ghazal has left you everything he owned."

"Everything?" Dan whispered as he looked around the store. Everything. Every book that reminded him of Saba. Every new fixture Dan had put in. Each freshly stained bookcase. There had hardly been a corner in *Olde Mysterium* that had gone untouched during Dan's renovations. To be honest, he just thought that it would all end one day and he would move on, finding something else to do. But he felt too strongly rooted. "This store is mine?"

Deborah nodded. "And more."

"There's more?"

"Saba owned this entire block. The offices, the stores, Billy Pints' bar—"

"Billy Pints?"

She affirmed. "It's all yours now."

Dan ran his fingers through his hair, now even more confused. He wanted to grieve the loss of his father, but something blocked the sorrow—a profound sense of gratitude. The old man had been nothing less than generous to Dan for a year, but this was Saba's *coup de grace*.

Deborah took up her satchel and stepped back. "I'll stop in another time for coffee, right now it seems you've got a lot of thinking to do...be sure to read the letter." She winked and then turned on her heels to leave.

"Wait. What about you? Didn't he leave you anything?"

"Yes he did. But it's not something that can be outlined in a will of last testament."

"I know what you mean, but still..."

A single tear ran down Deborah's cheek. "He paid my tuition through graduation for law school. He wanted to give me more, but I told him it wasn't necessary. I had to beg him not to." And with that she left the store.

Dan sat motionless, staring for several minutes at the envelope bearing his name. Gingerly, he lifted it and held it between his hands before breaking the seal to open it and pulling out the letter:

My Dearest Daniel,

There are precious few words that can describe the tremendous joy you have provided me in my last days upon this earth. Watching you grow into a man of love and compassion was awe-inspiring and the opportunity to support you was an honor. I am proud to call you my son forevermore.

Saba

CHAPTER TWENTY THREE

DAN'S EYES TRAVELED out of the passenger side window, watching the rhythmic flashing of the trees. The past couple of weeks had been some of the hardest he'd ever known, and yet he made it through unbroken in his spirit.

"Are you feeling all right?" The sweet voice sounded from the driver, Bridgette.

Dan pulled himself away from the window and looked at his wife and then down at her ever growing baby bump, and he couldn't help but smile. "Yeah I'm fine. There's just a lot to process." He sat up straighter and adjusted his tie. A tie. Daniel hadn't worn a tie since...well even he couldn't remember the last time he wore a *tie*. But of all occasions, by God this was the one where he was going to do it right.

He watched the road and pointed to Bridgette where to turn. They were getting close and he could feel the knots tighten in his stomach. The priest, Father Abu, had contacted Daniel a few days earlier and helped arrange the funeral service. Daniel placed the obituary in the Seattle Times as well as the Post-Intelligencer. He also insisted that Dan stand up to speak a few words on behalf of Saba. Dan agreed to it but not without trepidation.

"It's right up there," Dan spoke and motioned to the church coming into view. It was the same church that he had attended with Saba, the same building the Melkite Church community used to gather even though it was rented through the Catholic Diocese.

"I've never been to a Catholic Church," Bridgette whispered. "It looks very plain."

And Dan agreed that it looked very plain indeed. As they drove closer to the church, he could see cars parked all down the street and people getting out of their vehicles, making their way toward the church. Bridgette found a spot to park and they both began to make their way with the rest of the crowd.

Dan's eyes studied the crowd flowing toward the unremarkable church building. He couldn't even begin to count how many people there were and began wondering if they were all here for the same thing. The mass of people grew thick as they slowed at the entrances to the church. Father Abu stood outside greeting people as they filed in when he caught Daniel's eye and called him over. The priest then ushered Daniel and Bridgette down the center aisle toward the front pew and motioned for them to sit.

Dan glanced about and recognized sitting immediately around him the regular Melkite parishioners he had seen at the various church events. They too saw Daniel and either waved or nodded their respects in his direction. There was no coffin as the official burial had taken place earlier in the week and Saba had been laid to rest next to his son Joshua and Dan had done everything to make sure it was all in keeping with Saba's wishes and the tradition of the Melkite community. All of that had been small and efficient, and Father Abu had been extremely helpful. This was just supposed to be a memorial service, yet now Dan finally felt his nerves fraying at their ends. His eyes glanced backward and saw that seating had run out and the sides and back of the church were lined with standing onlookers. There were people packed out of the doors standing on their tip toes trying to look in.

On the table at the front of the church was a silver cross erected between two candles and a plate of knotted bread with three candles in it. The liturgy began and Father Abu went about the sanctuary performing all the rites that Daniel had previously witnessed when attending with Saba, but to his surprise the priest performed it all in English. He had watched the Melkite mass many times before but never understood what they were saying, yet now he was grateful to Father Abu for having the foresight to make it accessible to all who were visiting.

Father Abu stood to the front and said, "Let us ask the mercies of God, the Kingdom of Heaven, and the forgiveness of his sins, and the dwelling with Christ, our immortal King and God. Let us pray to the Lord."

"Lord, have mercy," the response came mostly from the Melkite parishioners, but was soon joined by everyone.

Father Abu then obtained a silver censer, which he began swinging lightly and a light colored aromatic smoke rose up from it and started to fill the sanctuary. "O God of all spirits and of all flesh, who have destroyed death, overcome the devil, and given life to the wold: grant, O Lord, to the soul of Your servant Saba who has departed from this life, that he may rest in a place of light, in a place of happiness, in a place of peace, where there is no pain, no grief, no sighing. And since You are the gracious God and lover of mankind, forgive him every sin he has committed by thought, or word, or deed, for there is no one who lives and does not sin: You alone are without sin, Your righteousness is everlasting, and Your word is true. For You are the resurrection and the life, and the repose of Your departed servant Saba, O Christ our God, and we render glory to You, together with Your eternal Father and Your All-holy, Good and Life-Giving Spirit, now and always and forever and ever."

"Amen," the people responded.

The choir sang a lovely but solemn tune and was followed by the Hierarch stepping into place up front and reciting, "You are the only immortal One, O Creator and Maker of man. We are mortals: out of the earth we were fashioned and to the same earth we shall return, as you have said and ordered, O my Maker: *Dust you are and to the dust you will return*. We all go down to the dust singing: Alleluia, Alleluia, Alleluia."

Dan's mind began to wander and his thoughts returned to the memories that were formed in the last year with Saba. A short vision of them sitting on top of the store's roof, smoking cigars and sipping whiskey pleased Daniel deep inside. The old man always joked about his death, but in the end he never really took it seriously even though he knew it came to reap him from this world. Saba's sights were always upon life and living, and trying to let everyone around him know that it was worth living. Always. Dan refocused in time to hear the service begin to come to the close.

"...and may He establish in the mansions of the just the soul of His departed servant Saba," Father Abu said.

"Amen," came the response.

"Grant him rest in the bosom of Abraham."

"Amen."

"And number him among the saints."

"Amen."

"For he is good and loves mankind."

"Memory eternal!" The crowd responded three times in a row.

Father Abu closed with the final prayer and then looked at Daniel with a wink. "Everyone here has come because Saba affected their lives in one positive way or another. But I don't think that many of you know he has a surviving son. Daniel, please come up here and speak your peace to us all."

Bridgette squeezed Daniel's hand and then he rose from his seat, stepped up on the dais, and turned to face the church. The crowd grew since Dan saw it last. Every door was open and nothing could be seen beyond them but heads of people trying to watch what was going on inside. His eyes raked the audience for familiar faces. Billy Pints caught his eye and nodded acknowledgement. Cinnamon and Tank sat in the midsection looking splendid in the best clothes they owned. Her short, natural brown hair had been styled for the occasion and Dan thought it looked divine. And then his eyes caught a fleeting sight amidst the lake of faces and saw Dodger peeking through in the crowd beyond the main sanctuary door. Dan could tell he had tried to clean himself up for the service, but his unwashed hair betrayed him even though Dodger had made an obvious attempt to comb it and his rough worn, beaten leather jacket announced the weathered life itself had lived.

Then Dan's gaze seized upon that of his wife; her eyes glistening with encouragement for her husband. At that moment the courage from within his pounding chest seized his nerves. "There's not much I can say about Saba Ghazal that many of you don't already know. He was a man who, from all appearances, devoted his life to his books and the study of knowledge. Yet to the discerning eye that was all a ruse, for Saba truly devoted himself to a life of love in servitude to any who were willing to accept his generous offers of service."

Nods and murmurs of affirmation arose from the onlookers. Every eye and every ear were upon him.

"In fact I probably knew Saba the least amount of time of anyone here, but he took me in during my darkest days. He gave me an opportunity to work and be useful again. He treated me like an old friend to whom he owed a large favor. I witnessed him offer charity to those in need. I forged friendships with those whom he helped. I saw Saba Ghazal share the deepest chambers of his heart by showing love to people whom the world would deem unlovable. Those throw-away-people became some of his favorite friends.

"Saba and I shared many cups of coffee and many great conversations over this last year of his life, but it was the first year of the beginning of my own. He helped me to break down my emotional and spiritual blockades. He knew that my own father had been a cruel and petty man and that it had affected me in ways I had yet to realize. But he loved me anyway. Saba saw that I had been wrapped up in the pursuits of my own personal glory and that my very natural drive for a prestigious career, the large house, the fast car, financial stability and security were nothing more than a husk to cover my emptiness. But he loved me anyway. He knew that my growing anger and indifferent responses to my wife's pleas to mend our marriage would eventually tear my soul apart. Yet he continued to shower me with an unconditional love that I can only explain as supernatural, for it is a gift that no man has at birth, but as I have learned from Saba, supernatural love is a gift that can be given to whomever asks for it. It is an unnatural love. It is an unconditional love. And it is ultimately necessary if we are to make this world a better place. And so he showed me the greatest kind of love I needed—Saba Ghazal made me his son, and I have accepted that completely.

"If Saba's life message were wrapped up in a motto, it might go something like this: Every life has value. Every soul is priceless. And every heart is broken. Saba's message challenges us all. Who among us has the courage to release our pain unto forgiveness and pursue those broken hearts in our midst so that they might know love? Who is willing to shoulder the cross of Christ to bring hope to the weary, the weak, and those in despair? Jesus Christ alone can heal the broken hearted, but those whom he heals are called to become like him and love a world of people lost in their own torment.

"Who is willing? I am willing. My name is Daniel, the son of Saba. And if any one of you should make your way into *Olde Mysterium*, I will have a pot of coffee brewing for just such an occasion...because that is how my father would want it."

Dan's eyes raked the silent room and eventually fell upon Dodger standing outside the sanctuary door, in the cold, with his jacket lapel flipped up against his neck. Their eyes met only for the briefest moment before Dodger pulled his gaze away and then left.

Daniel stepped down and sat by Bridgette, who reached her hand over and squeezed his own in embrace. Father Abu again went back up and finished the memorial service but Dan could not think upon it. The image of Dodger standing outside the church in the cold sent chills up Daniel's back. Dodger's eyes betrayed all: weary, weak, and in despair.

CHAPTER TWENTY FOUR

DAN ROLLED OVER in bed and looked at Bridgette, sleeping fast on her side. Her belly grew out to the point where she could no longer sleep on her stomach, which Dan knew to be her favorite sleeping position, but it didn't seem to bother her now. He rolled again onto his back and stared up at the ceiling. The memorial service had been a big deal and afterward had been even bigger with the reception. A full spread of home cooked dishes were provided by the parishioners of the church, but there was more than enough food to go around and all of it was amazing. He thought about all the people he spoke to, the faces he had seen, and the words of comfort Dan shared with those who came up to him. It felt like he interacted with everyone after the service...except Dodger. And that bothered him.

He rose from the bed and pulled open the curtain, watching the snow drift slightly but straight down. Here Dan slept comfortably in his house which was warm and full of love, yet something disturbed his spirit. Where would Dodger sleep tonight?

Dan could not shake the feeling that his friend was out there in the cold somewhere. He again checked on Bridgette, who continued to doze, and he then put on his jeans and bundled up for the weather outside. He knew something was wrong. Dan felt it in his core. And he was going to find Dodger because he knew that kid was sleeping on a sidewalk somewhere in Pioneer Square.

The car started up after two turns of the ignition and thumped to life, but needed a few minutes to grow into a warm rumble. Dan bowed his head. "Holy Spirit, I ask you to help me find Dodger tonight. Guide my driving to find your child."

Dan pulled away from the curb and made his way down the steep slopes of Queen Anne hill and into the heart of Seattle itself. His eyes kept watch through the snowy streets, but they were as empty as could be upon his first glance. Yet something continued to tug at his heart and he continued the slow sojourn. As he approached Pioneer Square, Dan could see lumpy tarps or newspapers piled into the store front doorways every block or so. He knew people were sleeping underneath the garbage to keep warm.

Dan parked behind *Olde Mysterium* and turned himself out on foot into the cold streets. The lamplights above glowed, making the snow that much more radiant. His eyes glanced into a storefront and saw a bundle of sleeping bags. He breathed deep and then approached the huddled mass. "Excuse me..."

The bags shuffled and a stocking capped head with a pair of eyes yellowed at the whites beneath it barely emerged.

Dan didn't even wait for a response. "I'm looking for Dodger, have you seen him?"

The bundled man thought a moment. "Nope, but I hope he made it into the shelter."

"Thanks," Dan said and turned away and then spoke under his breath, "me too." However the feeling inside insisted otherwise. He found another man sleeping beneath the black iron pergola but received a similar response. Dan walked through the square, down every side street, and through each alley he could pass through, but all the responses were the same. There was no sign of Dodger.

"Maybe he made it into the shelter tonight," Dan muttered, but his heart dropped because he knew it not to be true. Dodger was too independent sometimes, but the biting cold weather reminded Dan of the fact that everyone needs a friend...even a stubborn kid like Dodger.

Dan tromped on through the snow and then turned down an alley where he knew the homeless would gather on occasion. There was no light shining from above, but the snow lit up the darkness all the same. At the end of it, Dan stopped and looked but there was no one. He wondered where to go next, but then he heard a muffled sound come from a dumpster. Dan reached his hand out and lifted the lid, his eyes scanning the wasted newspapers, cartons, cans and other rubbish which shuffled a bit. Something was beneath it all.

"Hello in there. Could you help me? I'm looking for Dodger."

The trash shifted again and a head popped through, looking at Daniel. Dodger's young face and wispy beard were right there, and his blue eyes looked perplexed. "Dan? What are you doing here?"

"I'm looking for you. I...never got to talk to you after the memorial."

Dodger looked down the alley and then back at Dan. "And you want to talk now?"

Dan shrugged his shoulders. "Why not? Let's get you out of there. How would you like some coffee?" His eyes looked at the dark sky. "Decaf, of course."

Dodger nodded and then reached out his hand. Dan helped him out of the dumpster and they walked out of the white frosted alley and made their way toward *Olde Mysterium*. Dan pulled out his keys and unlocked the front door, ushering in Dodger.

"I can't believe Saba left you this place," Dodger said under his breath.

"I can't believe it either," Dan spoke and motioned for Dodger to follow upstairs. He showed Dodger the apartment above the store and led him to the bathroom, where he gave his friend a fresh towel. "How would you like to take a shower and get warm? I'll go downstairs and brew us some coffee."

Dodger simply nodded and took the towel. Dan went downstairs and started the coffee pot and then went back upstairs. He made sure he heard the shower running before opening the door and replacing Dodger's filthy clothes with a clean robe. Dan then took the clothes and began a cleaning cycle in the apartment's washer.

Downstairs, he poured out the coffee in two mugs and then sat at the table, waiting. Not long thereafter, Dodger came shuffling down the stairs wearing the robe.

"I took the liberty of washing your clothes. I hope you don't mind," Dan said, motioning to the seat across the table.

Dodger took the seat and sipped the black coffee. Dan nodded at the cream and sugar on the table, but Dodger shook his head. "Why are you doing this?"

Dan looked down at his hands. "I'm not sure. After the memorial earlier today, I just began to wonder where you went. Tonight I couldn't sleep, wondering where you were sleeping."

"Okay. So why are you doing this?"

Dan couldn't formulate an answer. He knew what he felt but he couldn't say it.

Dodger sipped the coffee. "Is it charity? Are you doing this because you feel I need help?"

Dan shook his head. "Do you need help?"

"No."

"That's what I thought. You've been taking care of yourself for a very long time, haven't you Dodger?"

Dodger nodded, his eyes fixed upon his mug.

Daniel sighed. "I'm doing this because, well I suppose...I need help. I need your help, Dodger."

Dodger's blue eyes perked up, looking at Daniel. "What?"

"This bookstore is too big for me to take care of alone. I know you like to read. I know you're smart.

And I know that you are my friend. Will you help me run *Olde Mysterium?*"

Tears formed in the corner of Dodger's eyes. "Sure but..."

"I'll pay you for your work. That apartment upstairs is yours, if you take the job. There are many valuable books in here and I need help to maintain them until they sell. During the day you'll help on the floor. At night, just live above the store to keep it safe. Deal?"

A single drop of water ejected from Dodger's eye and ran down his cheek, leaving a watermarked trail. "Deal."

Daniel stood up and stuck out his hand. "Thank you Dodger. You won't regret it."

Dodger shook Dan's hand. "Call me Tim. Tim Sorenson. It's—my real name."

Dan smiled. "I'll see you in the morning Tim."

EPILOGUE

DING. THE FRONT door bell chime hovered above the bookcases. Tim popped his head around from behind one of the shelves. "Dan! Visitors for you!" He smiled at Bridgette as he continued to shelve books and take inventory. Tim's weathered features had softened over the past several months. His beard was gone and replaced by a rounder, younger face.

"Send them back," Dan's reply called out from somewhere behind the book stacks.

He rolled his eyes. "Go on. You know where he is."

Bridgette nodded her thanks to Tim. "Is he still sitting at the computer?"

"Hasn't left. He just keeps staring at the monitor. I don't even know what he's trying to do in there."

He's grieving, Bridgette thought. Dan had been so busy keeping the store going, getting Tim acclimated to his new job, and garnering a fresh support of customers since the funeral that he had no left over moments in his day to grieve his own personal loss.

A loud hiss of steam escaped from the espresso bar to Bridgette's right. A couple of fresh faced college students poured hot, black shots into cups before adding the steamed milk. One barista noticed Bridgette and smiled, "What would you like today?"

"Nothing yet, Janine. But I'll be back."

Janine nodded and then looked at the bundled cargo Bridgette carried. "Is Joshua letting you get any sleep?"

Bridgette nodded. "A little, but we both get great naps in during the day."

"Well, that's a blessing in itself," Janine said.

"Yes, he certainly is." Bridgette crossed the floor of the store, pleased to see customers browsing the bookshelves. These people were drawn to the store more by the coffee and atmosphere than by the old books, but at least they were browsing with interest. She stopped by the office door and peeked in. Dan's back faced her as he sat, looking at a blank document on his monitor. "Knock knock."

Dan turned to look at Bridgette. She could tell he was sad but at the same time there was an immense peace surrounding him. It occurred to her that she had never seen his eyes so crystalline and happy. "Hey there beautiful. I see you brought my other favorite person," he said.

Bridgette handed over her small burden. "Joshua told me today that he wanted to see his Daddy."

"Well, I am so glad for that, Joshua." Dan gazed upon his son. His heart glowed with pride every time he said that name: Joshua. Bridgette had suggested the name when he was born to honor both Saba and his son. The boy opened his eyes and stared up at Dan. Joshua was almost three months old and his eyes were turning gray.

"How's it going in here?" Bridgette asked.

Dan sighed and shrugged. "I don't know. I feel like I'm supposed to do something. Feel something. Write anything. It feels like I just need to write but I don't know what say."

Bridgette ran a finger through her hair and closed her eyes. "Don't they say that you should start by writing what you know?"

"They? They talk a lot," Dan chuckled.

"Yes, I suppose they do. But I'm trying to get at something, Daniel."

"What's that?"

"You've been on a journey through this last year. Start by writing what you know. You have a story to tell." Her blue eyes opened with fresh tears in them. She leaned over and planted a kiss on Daniel and then took back Joshua.

"Write what I know?"

"Yes."

"But I barely—"

"Just start, okay?"

Daniel nodded and watched Bridgette and Joshua leave the office. He turned back toward the blank, open document; the curser blinking at him. *Write what I know*, he thought. But where to start? He sighed, closed his eyes, placed his fingers on the keyboard and began to type:

CHAPTER ONE

The face looking back at Daniel was grizzled, unshaven, and sad...

CPSIA information can be obtained at www.ICGtesting.com
Printed in the USA
BVOW01s0311040614

355106BV00002B/2/P